22 Letters

By Salem Miles

22 LETTERS

First edition. July 15, 2023.

ISBN: 979-8223945932

Written by Salem Miles.

Table of Contents

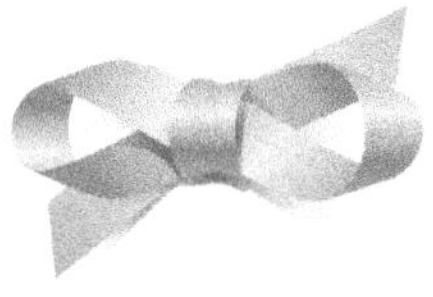

Acknowledgements

To the ones that need to hear this: you'll find the people that love you for you and will actually celebrate your uniqueness.

Chapter 1: The Bet

"Come on Leo, it's your turn!" Matthew groans, throwing the stack of cards down on the table.

Heaven knows I didn't want to come to Matt's house, and heaven knows very well that I didn't want to hang out with Derek's friends. Being around the popular kids of the 10th grade has never been on my to do list. But, because I'm a fan of stepping outside the box, I decided to take the risk once Derek brought that idea to the table. Derek has always wanted to see me succeed, and ever since he found out that I had a crush on Nathaniel, he's been doing everything in his power to set us up. And it looks like today, he's succeeded, because I actually came to hang out with Derek and the group of jocks, even though we have nothing in common. Heaven knows I could've been home.

But heaven also knows that I came for Nathaniel Daniels.

Nathan swipes back his fluffy blonde hair from covering his eyes as he grins at me. "Go on, Leon. It is your turn anyway," he says softly.

"Derek, remind me why we invited him again?" Jared asks, sighing. "We've done nothing but play cards all day."

"Yeah, Derek," adds Matt. "He can't play FIFA, so what can we do with him? We don't want him to feel left out."

"Are you sure we should be talking about Leon when he's right there?" Derek rolls his eyes. "Have some respect, please."

"Yeah guys, respect the captain of the chess team!" Thomas mocks me as I look down, the embarrassment coming over me for the second time today. "Maybe he'll teach us how to play chess or something."

"Alright, that's enough," Nathan surprisingly chimes in. "I'd rather play chess with Leon than watch you guys play FIFA any day and any time of the week. Leave him alone."

"Whatever," Jared mumbles. "We don't even know him that well anyways."

"That's why I invited him here, right Lee?" Derek asks and I nod in response. "I wanted you guys to know him better. He is my friend after all."

"He's really shy though," Thomas comments. "Maybe you shouldn't have brought him here."

"I'm not that shy," I murmur, earning a snicker from Matt.

"Yeah right."

"He really isn't." Derek came to my rescue.

"Prove it."

Derek and I exchange nervous glances as I gulp, forcing myself to look at Matt. "Want to bet on it?"

Surprised, Matt smirks at his crew. "Hear that, guys? Leon wants to bet on it."

"Oh wow," Derek utters under his breath.

"What, Adams? Want to speak up for your friend again?"

I lift my hand to stop Derek from speaking. "I can speak for myself."

"Fine, if you can, mind telling us who the lucky girl in your life is?"

Chuckles came from around the room as everyone's attention was on me, including Nathan's. Sighing, I shake my head. "I don't have one, I'm too scared to tell them that I like them."

"*Them*?" Thomas raises his eyebrows before it dawns on him. "Leon, are you–"

"Moving right along." Derek clears his throat, nudging Thomas. "How about this; I bet you can't tell your crush how you feel in a month's time."

"Really, dude? That's the best you could come up with?" Matt rolls his eyes. "Anyone can do that."

"But you guys assume he's the nerdy kid at school, so he can take the bet I gave him," Derek smiles at me, but his grin quickly disappears once he sees the anger and embarrassment on my face. "What? I didn't lie. Someone had to tell you one way or another."

"You know what? I'll take that bet."

"Shocking."

"And what happens if Leon doesn't tell their crush how he feels?" Nathan asks.

"Well he'll have to run around the hallways wearing a clown costume at school; that's what he has to do," Matt laughs. "And it doesn't matter if he gets rejected; all he has to do is ask his crush, and provide proof of it, including the answer. All this within a month."

"That's so easy, I can even do this before the month ends," I bluff, smirking at Matt. "You could've given me less."

"Alright then; 24 days." He shrugs. "But there's a catch."

"What's the catch?"

"You can only tell them in the last 2 days," he announces, and my smirk drops. "What? Are you backing out already?"

"No, I—" once my eyes met Nathan's, I forced a grin onto my face. "You could've been a little harder than that, Matthew. I thought that Matthew the jock would go a little stronger on my bet, instead of acting like a little—"

"A little what, James?" He stands up, his hands turning into fists.

"Calm down, Matt," Nathan orders. "He was kidding."

"24 days, Matthew." I smirk, the false confidence masking up my anxiety faster than Usain Bolt could ever run. "24 days."

Now the question here remains; *how the fuck am I going to tell Nathan in 24 days?*

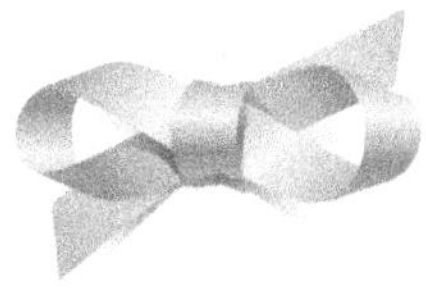

Chapter 2: What To Do

"You did *what*?" Cecelia hit Derek's arm as she slammed her locker shut. Cecelia Williams is the last person in our trio that has existed since our freshman year in 2021. She's a petite brunette with brown eyes and a skinny frame. Cece and I bonded in 2021 over our shared love for chess, and we've been best friends ever since. Derek and I, on the other hand, got stuck in school on the night of the school play, waiting for our parents to arrive and pick us up. We got to talk during that time, and became friends after a while.

"Derek, you stupid fuck." Cecelia punches his arm slightly while he yelps.

"Hey! What's your problem?" He whines, rubbing his arm.

"Why the hell would you force Leon to tell Nathan he likes him? Are you stupid?" Cece slams her hand against the locker hard, causing the passing students to check the commotion.

"Hey, it was his decision to agree to the bet." Derek murmurs, closing his locker and facing us again. "It's not my fault that Leon thinks he's so tough."

"I only agreed because Nathan looked interested in the bet!" I sigh. "It's not my fault that he looked so intrigued by it."

"See? You got into this on your own." He shrugs. "Besides, how are you gonna do it anyways?"

"Tell Nathan I like him? I have no idea." I glance over at Nathan, who's across from us. "I'm pretty sure I'm not his type of guy. Or maybe, I'm just not his...you know."

I point at Nathan, who's talking to a petite, blonde girl. She laughs at what he's saying, dropping her pen so that she could pick it up, all while Nathan seems a little uncomfortable with the suggestive nature of her action.

"Shouldn't have agreed," Derek mutters.

"You shouldn't have given him such a bet. You know how shy Leon is." Cece flicks my forehead. "You're literally putting this guy in check."

"Can't put me in check if you only have one piece," I counter, winking at Cece.

"Stop with the chess jokes, it's seriously getting on my nerves," Derek scoffs. "Besides, Leon was being pressured by Matt. If I didn't say something, he would've been given a worse bet than I actually gave him. I also blame him for acting a little tough for nothing towards the end; he suggested a smaller time-line than the one I gave him."

"First of all, I wasn't acting tough for nothing, I just wanted to show off to Nathan how confident I am." I smile.

"So, in short, you just showed Nathan how bad of a liar you are?" Cece quips.

I frown. Maybe it wasn't such a good idea to agree to a bet. That means finding confidence that I scarcely have, to man up and tell Nathan how I feel. That means stepping out of my comfort zone, and being a little more...open. This is the shit Derek puts me into.

Or rather, the shit that I put myself into.

"I can give you a headstart, Leo." Derek smiles. "Julia's gone, go talk to Nate."

"Why are you helping me?"

"Because I'm your damn friend, and I personally don't want to see you run around in a clown costume." Derek shudders. "Go talk to him, Cece and I will wait here for you."

I nod as Derek gives me my books. Sighing, I walk over to Nathan, and stand by his locker, trying to figure out what to say. He continues to put his books in the lockers, barely noticing me, so I clear my throat so that he can focus, and when he finally does look at me, he beams.

"Hey, man." He gives me a hug as I accidentally inhale his cologne.

This man is literal heaven. He smells like a thousand flowers in the garden of Eden.

Okay, my exaggeration.

"How are you? I've been meaning to tell you that you're actually really brave for taking a bet like that. I could never tell my crush how I feel." Nate compliments me.

"Thanks, Nate..." I trail off as his hand gently brushes mine. "I was wondering if I could get some advice on something?"

I have to be subtle about this. There's no way I can win the bet without actually getting information from the crush themselves. He probably doesn't know it's him, so it's easier this way.

"Yeah?"

"How would you get your crush to notice them? I mean, you're one of the best juniors out here and you can get any girl you possibly want, but I can't," I explain. "How would you tell them?"

"First of all, you're a good looking guy, you can get anyone you want too. And second of all, I'm really cheesy." He says sheepishly. "I do like someone confident, but at the same time I would do something cringey or unpredictable. Like, le-"

The bell rings, startling Nathan before he could get the chance to finish what he was saying. "I'm sorry, I have to go for physics now. Good seeing you, James." He scurries away, disappearing into the halls.

What was he about to say? Was he going to say leverage over the situation? Leaflets? Lemonade?

I wave at Derek and Cece as they make their way to the class while I go up the stairs. Deciding to stop by the library, I sat in my usual spot and took out my notepad. I began to scribble down possible ideas of telling Nathan how I like him; ideas that won't have me embarrassed or in tears.

Frustrated, I throw the paper with useless ideas away into the dustbin, while staring at the blank page. While playing with my pen, I gasped, as a new idea came to mind.

"What if..." Setting the tip of the pen neatly on the paper, I begin to write, putting my new plan into motion.

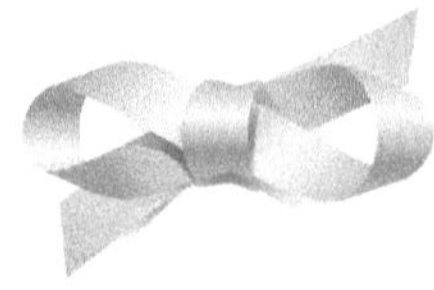

Chapter 3: Letter Number 1

"Nathan said he likes something cheesy? Now imagine how cheesy this letter is going to be," I mutter to myself.

It's your secret admirer.

I groan, tearing the page and throwing it in the bin as well. That's stupid *and* cheesy. I need something more unique to myself, something that would stand out of the crowd.

Giving it another shot, I began to write the letter a little more seamlessly.

You probably don't know me. You can just call me J. I'm not the type of person you'd go for, which is why I'm writing my thoughts down instead of confronting you.

I've seen you around, I know who you are, Nathan. This might seem stalkerish, and you might throw this away, but I just want to let you know how much I care about you.

You are different. You're not like the other popular guys, you're actually nice to me. It's funny because being nice to somebody like me is kind of weird and unexpected, which is how I know that you are different.

Anyways, back to what I was saying. I've seen you around and I actually think you're a pretty great person. If you're wondering who this is, you'll probably never know. I don't even know why I'm doing this.

Have a beautiful day Nathan, this isn't the last you've heard from me....

Signing out,

J

I fold up the paper and stand, walking towards the librarian to ask if I can go to my locker. Once she's said yes and I'm down the stairs, I scan the halls for Nathan's locker while biting my lip, feeling nervous.

"Maybe I shouldn't do this," I whisper to myself as I stare at his locker. "Nathan isn't dumb. I shouldn't do this but..." I pause, closing my eyes briefly. "But I don't think I *have* a choice at the moment."

This may be the only discreet way of winning this bet.

I take a deep breath then slip the note into his locker, whistling slowly as I hear the piece of paper drop inside, sealing the deal. Is this a good idea? Probably not. Should I have done this? Again, probably not.

But I guess that's too late now.

I rush back to the library and sit back down,

This is probably the only way I can address my feelings for Nathan. He won't know it's me, plus I'm being completely authentic. But what if he doesn't like it? What if he sees it and immediately report me for this?

Day one of this letter business and so far I feel so guilty and stupid.

"It's too late now anyways, I guess I have to wait and see his reaction," I mumble to myself, opening my geography textbook.

Chapter 4: Stalker Alert!

I stare at Nathan as he places the letter on the table and picks up his taco. I never thought he'd open the letter at lunch, but here he is; trying to figure out why there was a letter in his locker.

"Earth to Leon."

I snap out of it, and lock eyes with Derek and Cecelia, who shake their heads simultaneously. "Is that how you plan on telling him?"

"No, it's just that..." I glance at Nathan again, who's still eating his taco in peace as he waits for Matt and the rest to surround the table. "I may or may not have sent him a letter."

"Wait, that was you?" Derek laughs. "I knew it!"

Cece narrows her eyes at me. "What do you mean you *sent him a letter*?"

"I slipped a letter in his locker when you guys went for your classes," I explain, smiling sheepishly as Cece's expression changes from amusement to pure and utter horror. "I know what it sounds like, but I promise you it wasn't as weird as it seemed at the time."

"Stalker much?" Cece rolls her eyes. "Of all the things you could've done, Leon, and you decided to be a mailman?"

"Hey, you know how socially anxious Leon gets," Derek defends me. "And you shouldn't be talking. You always talk about this guy that you like, but you can never get with him, so shut it till you have the actual balls to talk to him."

"I'm a girl and if you didn't know, girls have vag—"

I chuckle to myself as the duo bicker, knowing that Cece has a crush on Derek, and he has feelings for her as well. She thinks I don't know, but she's made it obvious at this point with her starry eyes around him and how her face looks like an inflated tomato when he's around her. It would be weird if they dated, but as long as the friend group doesn't dissolve if they break up, then I'll be cool with it. Either way, I have no say in this, and it's none of my business.

I have my own fish to fry anyway.

I watch as Nathan finally picks up the letter and opens it. Matt tries to peek at the letter, but Nathan moves away from him, glaring at him. His eyes land on the paper again, and his cheeks begin to tint pink as he reads, my heart skipping a beat once he smiles. He then shakes his head, and slips the letter in his bag, his attention back on his taco. In an instant, he looks up and catches me staring, confusion washing over his face as I awkwardly wave at him. He waves back, a small smile stretching on his face. But our moment gets interrupted as Matthew pats Nathan's back, grabbing his attention.

Matt's gaze then settles on me. And soon, he's walking to our table.

Derek and Cece's bickering stops once Matt reaches our table. He pulls himself a chair and faces me, a smirk on his face.

"Matt, leave." Derek quickly steps in before he can say anything. "I already know what you're here for."

"Come on, Derek. I just wanted to know how the bet is going," Matt says, sickeningly sweet. "How's everything lining up, Leon? Have you talked to them yet?"

"He has," Cece replies. "And he's making progress. Are you done now?"

"I'm sure Leon can speak for himself."

"Are you obsessed with him?" Derek laughs.

"Nope, just curious." Matt lays his hands on the table. "Nathan received a letter."

"So I've heard." I nod.

"Is it from you?"

"All the girls in this school and suddenly you think I would write him a letter? Literally everyone in Grade 10 worships the ground he walks on."

"I wouldn't be surprised if you do too," Matt adds. "I just find it funny how a letter suddenly comes in for him, days after I placed the bet with you. Coincidence?"

"Those happen sometimes."

"Matt, get a life and worry about yourself instead of worrying about Leon. He's doing the bet and he's winning the bet, what's your problem?" Derek groans.

"He's probably trying to confess his feelings to Leon," Cece jokes. "*Oh Leon, let's forget this challenge and run off into the sunset and make out–*"

"Alright, that's enough," Matt snaps. "I'm watching you, Leon." He gets up and walks back to his table, whispering into Nathan's ear. Nathan looks at me while Matt feeds him information, and he frowns, shoving Matt off of him.

"What's going on with him?"

"Matt thinks you're sending Nathan letters, so he's been teasing Nathan about it in class. It's been an interesting few hours."

"Do you think he's up to something?"

"I don't know." Derek shrugs.

"Okay, can you try and find out more? Maybe you can convince Matt to hop off of Leon's ass," Cece suggests while rubbing Derek's shoulder.

"On it." The bell rings, the end of break time dawning upon us. "I have physics class now. See you guys later." He stands, winking at me. "And Leon?"

"Yes?"

"Keep writing those letters. Don't mind Matt; just focus on how you're going to tell Nathan and nothing else."

"We believe in you, Leo," Cece stands as well, linking her arm with Derek's.

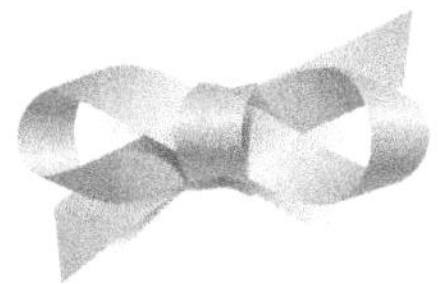

Chapter 5: Letter Number 2

Hey Nate, it's me again!

I noticed that you got my first letter, and I'm really sorry if it was weird or unusual; I just didn't know how to deliver it to you and thought of that as the safest option. I'm still delivering them through this method though, because I can't have you figuring out how I am so soon! There's no fun in that.

So how was your day? How are you?

I know you can't answer these questions because, well, you can't see me and you don't know me. Or maybe you do.

So, I've been doing my research and I've come to the conclusion that you really like flowers. Isn't that odd? Again, I'm giving stalker vibes, but I just realised that we have quite a bit in common.

Except I'm not really a runner, I'm more of a thinker.

So why I bothered you about your interest in flowers is because I love flowers too. There's a beautiful garden over on Winfrey Street, where roses, tulips and all sorts of flowers make their presence known. It's their home; it's where they belong.

There's just something comforting about realising that you are where you belong. All my life I used to search for that, but when I met my friend group and they opened their arms to me, I felt safe. I wonder if you know what it feels like to feel safe, and what it feels like to be home. I once read a book that had the quote, 'home is not a building, it's people' and it didn't make any sense till they came around.

Anyways, enough rambling.

I go to the garden to think. The serenity and quietness of the garden calms me, and it knows how to recharge my exuberant, introverted nature. I know you don't know where this garden is, and that makes me happy because you won't have to see my face anytime soon.

I'm smart, I know.

Anyways, I was walking in the garden yesterday and I picked up a tulip. It reminded me of you because to me, you're like a flower, you love to show the world your beauty, engulfing everyone with your kindness and charm.

While I was at it, I picked up another flower; a poppy.

I related it to myself. Some say I'm naive and oblivious to reality, while others say I have childlike innocence. I don't know which is which, but the poppy shows me that you can still manage to stand out in a garden full of tulips and red roses. Poppies still bloom, Nate, and that may not sound like anything to you, but it's everything to me.

I spend a lot of my time here because nature can take you to a different place if you truly let it. All it takes is a few seconds, and a sea of thoughts can turn into a mere shadow once the summer breeze hits your face. You should try visiting the garden sometime, it takes you into the unknown, and can truly calm your spirit if you let it.

I hope you take my advice one day. I'll talk to you tomorrow.

Signing out,

J.

I slip the letter into his locker once again and head to the gymnasium for P.E class. I walk into the locker room, throwing my bag down and sitting on the bench, looking at the ground as I get myself together.

"You're early."

When I look up to see who it was, my mouth drops. It's Nathan, and he's *shirtless*.

His cheeks turn rosy, and he scratches the back of his neck as he looks at me. "Why are you blushing?"

"Why are *you* blushing?" I mutter under my breath as I quickly look away from him.

"I—nevermind." he clears his throat. "So, remember that day you wanted advice?"

"Of course, you were saying something and then the bell rang–"

"Well, I had to think about what I wanted to say to you. You're a smart guy, and I didn't want to sound stupid in front of you," he rambles. "I was hoping we could talk about it over some lemonade."

I knew it!

"Of course. Maybe after school?"

Nathan nods, and pats my back. "Sure, dude. Do you have your phone on you?"

I quickly reach into my bag and give him my phone. He types his number in, and grins at me as he hands the phone back to me.

"We can hang out at Rocco's, my cousin works there and he could give us a discount."

"Of course!" I exclaim, covering my mouth as soon as the words slip out.

Nathan raises an eyebrow, but nonetheless chuckles. "You're funny."

At least he thinks I'm funny.

"I heard you have a secret admirer," I blurt out once I uncover my mouth.

"News spread that fast?" He frowns, but his facade returns just as fast as the frown appeared. "It's pretty funny actually."

"What is?"

"Having a girl do that for me–"

"Why are you assuming it's a girl?"

"Because they usually throw themselves at me in weird ass ways, even though I hate it," he explains. "I always dodge them though, I'm not really into girls like that so it would be awkward. Any girl would do this to get my attention, and I wouldn't be surprised if it was one."

"Expect the unexpected," I mutter.

"Do you know them by any chance? You seem a little weirded out by the fact that I said girls throw themselves at me." He cocks his head to the side.

"I don't," I lie. "And the bet is going okay; each day I'm making progress."

Nathan smiles. "That's good, I'm rooting for you all the way." he then sticks out his hand for me to take. "Are you ready to run a few laps?"

I laugh as he ruffles my hair. "Only if you are."

"Always ready."

Chapter 6: Lemonade and Tulips

I tap my fingers on the wooden table, patiently waiting for Nathan to come to Rocco's. I made sure to get here as early as possible so that I can look through the menu, as well as build up the confidence to have a conversation with Nathan outside of school. He took my number yesterday and did send me a message confirming if we were still on, and all I sent was a flimsy thumbs up. For a sixteen year old whose puberty is hitting slower than most, I somehow don't know how to talk to a boy. Heck, I probably don't even know how to act on a date.

It's not a date. *God, I know it's not a date.*

After a few minutes, Nathan shows up with a book and a pen. He takes a seat in front of me, signalling for a waiter to come. He then looks at me, a grin growing on his face as he winks. The waiter arrives, and Nate clears his throat.

"Welcome to Rocco's can I take your—Nate? Glad to see you here man!" The petite redhead with freckles laughed as she put her pad down. "It's been a while! Why haven't I seen you here? Or even back at my mom's house?"

"I've been busy with school, Nikki," he admits, nodding at her. "What time does your shift end? Maybe I can get you a few drinks after your round."

"There's no need, dude. I'm the older sister here, let me give you and your friend drinks, on the house," Nikki says, waving at me as she picks up her pad and clicks her pen. "What are we having today?"

Nathan hums. "Maybe the usual for me?" He shifts his gaze towards me. "What are you having, Leo?"

"Well...can I get some pink lemonade with a burger and fries?"

Nikki writes it down. "Alright, should be done in about fifteen minutes, wouldn't want to keep you waiting any longer."

Nathan looks up at her. "*Longer?*"

She chuckles. "Yeah, your friend has been here for over ten minutes, staring at his phone and the menu. I'm sure he's hungry." She then winks at me. "I'll be back."

Nathan cocks his head at me, eyes squinted as Nikki scurries off. "You got here early?"

"Yeah, I wanted to check out the vibe of this place before you got here," I lie smoothly, rubbing the back of my neck. "It's not as crowded as I thought it would be."

"Yeah, it's just after school though, so it's bound to get a little bit busier in about...now." He points to the door and I turn to look, watching as a couple of his own friends and some other kids come in. He rolls his eyes as Matt approaches our table and slams a paper down, shaking the table a bit.

"I told you I'd get a C!" He slams Nate's back before acknowledging my presence. "Oh...Leon."

"Hi."

His attention is back on Nate, who's glaring at him. "Of all the things I've seen you do, I never thought you'd hang out with chess boy."

Chess boy?

"Matthew..."

"No wonder Chelsea—"

"Matt!" Nathan snaps.

Matt raises his hands up in defeat. "I'm kidding."

"Leave the kid alone," Jared orders. "Nathan, have fun with...whatever this is, we're just here to get shakes and head home." Jared walks away.

"Don't forget to give Leon tips on how to flirt, rumour has it that chess nerds don't know how to—"

"Matthew!"

Groaning, Matt goes to Jared and the others, while I sit there shitting bricks; are they actually talking about me in their stupid little circle? If they are, *what in the world are they saying?*

"Leon?"

I'm pushed back into reality as Nathan gazes at me, concern written all over his face. I open my mouth to speak, but no words come out, so instead I look away and check my surroundings again as my breathing quickens at the thought of what they're saying about me, especially to Nathan.

"Hey, look at me."

Embarrassed, I meet his gaze, my lips pursed together tightly.

"Don't mind them, okay?"

I nod.

"Leon, listen to me; do not mind them," he repeats. "They're just stupid, they know nothing and even if they did, what are they going to do? Nothing. Just calm down, Leon."

Taking a deep breath, I smile a little, trying not to worry him. "I'm okay."

"You promise?"

"Yeah," I lie. "I do."

"Okay."

The food arrives and Nate immediately digs in while I patiently wait for my body to go back to normal. After a while, everything becomes normal again, and Nate picks up the conversation with me. We get to know each other a bit more; he's apparently the first born in a family of 3 kids. He has twin sisters, and his parents are almost never around. They always go on business trips and leave the kids with their nanny, as well as leaving Nathan as he's the only other parental figure to the twins.

I in turn tell him about my life; my Hispanic heritage and how my parents always prided themselves in being proudly Dominican, while I try to shy away from it sometimes. I pick my words carefully, trying to leave out how I met my best friends, as well as why I developed an interest in chess. It's not something I'd like to share with him, at least at the beginning stages of our friendship.

Or whatever he wants this to be. After all, he only agreed to meet me because of the bet.

"Lee?"

"*Lee?*"

He chuckles. "Yeah, I figured a lot of people call you Leon or Leo, so why can't I be the first one to call you Lee?" He smiles, his gaze sucking me in.

"Oh, I just thought of Lee from the kissing booth," I joke. "I thought you were comparing me to him."

"First of all, yes I am. And secondly, you watched The Kissing Booth? I thought guys didn't like the movies."

"Boys can like cheesy movies too," I quip. "Did you watch the first one only?"

"The whole trilogy, actually. Don't tell anyone this but..." he leans over the table. "I am still a Marco and Elle stan to this day."

"Me too! They had so much chemistry together, so for her to have the audacity to not go for him was insane."

"And the fact that she choose *neither* of them at the end of the last film was such a bummer. All that build up for nothing."

"They wanted her to have a girl boss moment and even tried to hint st her getting back with Noah," I explain. "Like, why can't the writers stick to one idea?"

Nathan laughs. "Wow, you're actually pretty funny."

"Thanks," I sheepishly say, sipping my lemonade.

"So, do you know where Winfrey Street is? There's this garden I'm looking for." I choke on my drink, immediately coughing. "Are you okay...?"

"Yeah, I am." I cough one last time before clearing my throat. "Why are you looking for it? Planning on going there?"

"You don't need to know why," Nate explains. "I just want to see the garden, that's all. I've heard amazing things about it."

"From who?"

"A friend."

"Oh okay." I sip the lemonade once more. "It's two streets away from here, just past Glenora Road. There's a gated community that you have to enter, then ask about the garden; it's free to all, as long as you're clean."

"Thank you."

"I might even take you there sometime, if you're up for it. I love going there," I add.

Nathan thinks for a minute, before nodding. "Maybe after your bet. That's if you win of course."

I laugh, and we start talking about other things. Turns out, Nathan and I do have quite a bit in common; chess, the inexplicable admiration of flowers, and coffee. He's always wanted to join the chess team, but because of athletics and his desire to remain captain for the junior athletics all the way into being captain when we become seniors, he dedicates most of his time to it.

To soften the mood, I offered to play chess with him sometime. Presumably over coffee, since that's what he likes.

Time flew between us, and it seemed as if we knew each other our whole lives. Somehow, that made me like him even more than I did before, and my stomach fluttered as Nate asked me to meet him at his party in a few weeks. This means he's starting to trust me, because Nate would *never* invite someone like me to a party unless he's cool with me being there. Or maybe I'm just putting him higher than everyone else.

I really need to stop being so fucking whipped.

I grab a hold of my phone and call Derek once Nate leaves. "Leonardo Dicaprio?"

Ignoring the nickname, I sigh. "I was just with him, Derry."

"Oh, that's...that's great." He's panting, and suddenly, he whistles. "Can I call you later, Leo? I'm kind of in the middle of something here."

"What are you doing?" I ask as I exit the restaurant, heading for the garden. "Or better yet, *who?*"

"I'm just chilling, you know me," he nervously laughs. "And I'm just—"

"Doing me, of course. Who else would he be doing?"

My mouth drops as Cecelia yells on the phone, and Derek immediately cuts it. I shake my head in disbelief; they're *doing* each other?

I mean, Cecelia likes to joke around about this stuff, and she's always told me that she wanted to wait before giving it up. Now that Derek suddenly, or maybe always has, likes her, she's all up for it? It's strange, but warranted. As long as they don't break each other's hearts in the end, like Derek has always been with the girls since last year, I don't mind.

I open the gate to the garden, and walk in. As I'm strolling through the flowers while letting nature take me in, something catches my eye; A paper taped to a tulip, and because I'm a curious idiot, I pick it up.

This is a long shot, and you probably won't read this if the wind is too strong and blows this fucking paper away, but I find you cute. I like how smart and cheesy you can be at the same time, J.

Nathaniel♡

Nathan...Nathan wrote back to *me? And used his full name too?*

Jumping around like a kid that was given candy after a punishment, I dance around on joy before stopping to put the letter in my pocket. Now, there's only one question that truly remains;

Should I continue writing these letters, or should I come out and tell him the truth?

Chapter 7: Letter Number 3

Okay, I definitely wasn't expecting you to reply, but since we're practically talking to each other through these letters;

How are you, Nate? Or should I say Nathaniel? What an adorable name for a future athlete.

I'm kidding. Okay, maybe I'm not. Whatever.

Since you told me your full name, there's no reason why I shouldn't tell you mine, right? Kidding, there's always a reason. However, I'll give you one more initial in my name. There's an E in it. Yes, an E.

Trust me, I'd love to tell you my entire name, but I'm just scared of the outcome on this, or how you would see me...you get the gist.

"Getting bold now, aren't we?" Cece raises her eyebrows at me.

"Whatever, Cece." I look at my paper again.

As I was saying, that's all I'm telling you for now.

Maybe I'll give you more initials when you're ready. Correction, when *I'm* ready.

So I'm just curious Nate, who are you really? When the athlete has gone home, when you're ready to be yourself at home without your friends cheering for you, who are you? Is this just an act, or is there more to the athlete every 10th grade girl is swooning over?

There has to be more.

I'm not saying you're bad or anything, or that you're playing pretend for the cameras, but there's always a hidden layer to someone. There's a side that we don't see, a side we hide from the world because we know it won't be accepted or loved as the one we've put to the world. There's even that side to me, but I want to know about you, and who you are when the curtains to your bedroom are closed, and you're in the comfort of your own bed.

I want to know the real you.

You may never know the real me, because the real me would have you disgusted...or even embarrassed. But only time will tell, and if I get more letters from you, then maybe I'll let you in on who J really is. Maybe I'll continue going to the garden, in hopes that my Eden (you) will be there.

And I secretly pray that you're there.

Well, till next time, my Eden.

If you didn't know, that's my nickname for you now. Do I hate it? No. Do I find it a bit cheesy? Maybe. But that doesn't matter anyway.

Signing out,

J.

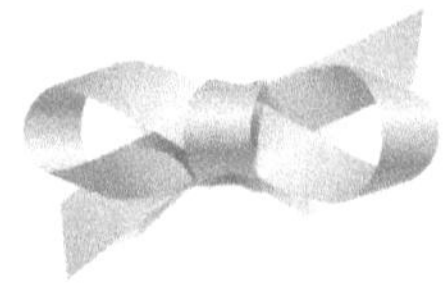

Chapter 8: La Lettre De Nathan

Hey J, or E, you confused me a little when it came to your alleged name. First of all, I'm okay. The reassurance from you keeps me going, and makes me a little happy. Secondly, there is a side that no one has ever seen of me, and I don't know if anyone ever will.

Plus, even if I tell you, there's a chance that you go to my school, and you'd probably tell everyone so that they'll make fun of me. Especially Matt, he'll have a proper reason to hate me.

But silly me is going to tell you anyway.

I don't know what I want. Like, romantically. It's a bit weird to me, but I think I'm attracted to both guys and girls. Bisexuality was something I've never thought of growing up, but now I might actually consider it because when I get around this one person, something just changes in me. It's like I get butterflies in my stomach when I think about them.

I don't know what I feel, and telling you is probably a bad idea, but I have no idea who to go to. My friend group is as toxic as ever, and I know they'll just laugh at me or get some girl to help me 'get over it' even though I don't want to.

Anyways, I'll just place this somewhere I know you'll see it. Also, keep breaking into my fucking locker and you and I might have a problem (wink wink).

Nathaniel♡

I re-read the letter about 10 times. Bisexual? Nathaniel is *bi*? So I *do* have a chance. Or maybe I don't. But I guess the only way I'll find out...is if I continue to write.

And that's what I'm going to do.

Chapter 9: Derek & Cecelia

They both shift in their seats, steadily avoiding eye contact as I flip through my notebook, waiting. I do have another letter to write for the fourth day, but sometimes, there are other things to deal with; like finding out when Derek and Cecelia suddenly became Derek *and* Cecelia.

"Since when?"

"What are you talking about?" Cecelia acts oblivious.

"Since when did...*this* happen." I wave my hand in between them. "Last time I was with you two, you were bickering over ice cream that wasn't even good."

"Hey, I like mint! Is that a crime?" Cecelia argues.

"It is a crime because everything you seem to like is either disgusting or unattainable!"

"Alright, alright, let's calm down now," Derek intervenes. "It hasn't been long, Leon, trust me on that one."

Cece scoffs. "Sure, a month isn't—"

"*A month*?"

"Cecelia!"

"How did a whole month go under my nose like that?" I ask them. "I'm literally always with you. Does...does anyone else know about this?"

"If you didn't know, then I'm sure no one else does. Derek treats me like his little sister, even though we're kind of dating."

"Interesting." I squint my eyes at Derek. "Hurt her and I'll hurt you."

"Leon."

"Alright guys, let's talk about something else. Are you coming for chess today? We have to practice for the tournament in April," Cece changes the subject.

"What tournament?" I ask.

"Well, if you had attended the meetings instead of tiptoeing around Nathan's dick, our school is hosting a chess tournament where one lucky student can stand the chance to win a gtadn prize of $1000. All schools in our league are eligible to enter, which is why it wouldn't be fair if our *captain* wasn't present. What do you think?"

"I'll come sign up today." I flip my notebook and grab a pen. "I hope you and Derek actually last, I know both your track records at this point."

"Leon I swear to—" The librarian is quick to hush him. "Sorry ma'am." He turned back to me. "I like her a lot, I'm sure we will."

"Hopefully." I put in my headphones and start to play 'Bellyache' by Billie Eilish while I write the letter. I have approximately 2 hours to get this letter into the garden, and approximately an hour before I bump into Nathan on *accident.*

Not on accident, by the way.

. . ✤ . .

NATHANIEL,

It's me again, the one and only.

I like that you took time out of your day to talk to me you know, it's actually quite cute. However, onto something, or rather someone, who is actually cute.

Just kidding, you're handsome, Nate. Don't even say you aren't, you'd be lying to me and yourself.

It's like you're the blonde version of Troy Bolton from High School Musical, just less cringe and much more caring. If you haven't watched High School Musical then I'm sorry you don't have a childhood, but if you have, then this should be something we should laugh over together.

Besides that, how was your day? I've been reading into your history at school(oh my God I'm such a stalker!) And noticed you actually did play chess at some point. Maybe one day, you'll become the King to my Queen.

And I'm on fire with the puns today!

Have a beautiful day my Sweet Eden (that will never get old, trust me) if you're lucky, I might write you a poem tomorrow. That's if, you'd want me to...wink wink.

See? I'm learning a new skill each and every day.

Signing out,

J

Chapter 10: Chess, Sports...and more Lemonade?

Cecelia only improved in chess in order to beat me, I have evidence. Number 1: she must have taken the time to memorize my movement patterns because everytime she makes a move, she smiles. The other reason I have this theory is because after every move I made, she asked if I was sure. Good move, just wrong person.

As usual, I scan the board and slowly smile as I find her king open and unguarded; you never leave the king unguarded.

I placed my final rook on the last square, watching Cece's jawdrop as she goes into checkmate.

"How?"

"Remember what I told you the first time we started playing. Never leave the king without another piece guarding it. Preferably two. That's the easiest way to get yourself into checkmate sometimes," I explain. "But good game, I can also tell you've been studying me a lot, so I think need to change my strategy, right?"

She grins. "No, don't change a thing."

"You know I won't—"

"No, Leon, you're not listening to me." She reaches for my hand. "Don't ever change a thing about yourself."

I frown, not sure of what she's talking about, until a hand suddenly drops on her shoulder. Looking up, Nathan looks down at her and nods.

"Mind if I get this round?"

Cece's bothered for only a moment, before she winks at me and gets up. Nathan and I start to rearrange the pieces, and once they're back in order, he flips the board to get the black pieces, which surprises me.

"Sorry, I hope that doesn't distract the *captain*, I like to watch my opponent move," he says as I shrug and continue to move.

"Nice one," I reply as he moves his knight first. *I've seen this before.*

"Wait! Before we continue." He reaches for something in his bag. "Pink lemonade! I noticed you liked it so I brought you some."

"You remembered?" I beam at him.

"Of course I did. Not everyday you find someone that shares the same pink lemonade addiction as you." He laughs.

Then followed moments of silence. As we played, I began to realize that Nathan wasn't a first time player. Why, you may ask?

He beat me in 25 moves.

"Wow." I gasp. "Good game, Nate. Good game."

"I reckon no one has beat you before?"

"Not at this school, no." I muse. "You should sign up for the tournament, you have a good chance of winning too."

Nathan sits back in his chair and thinks. "This would have to depend on the date and time. Extracurricular activities have been postponed on my end because of athletics."

"So how'd you come here?"

"Because you were here."

My breathing stops for a minute. "So?"

Nathan shrugs delicately, a grin on his face. "I wanted to see you."

"I don't know what to say."

"Don't say anything, I actually got myself into shit by coming today, but whatever. Totally worth it." He nods.

"What happened?"

"Coach. I told him that I was missing practice today to go do something, and he didn't like that at all," Nate explains, sighing. "It doesn't matter though, he needs to know that track isn't on my mind 24/7."

"Well, if you want to be captain, then it should be one of the most important things to you," I argue. "That's if, you don't want to be captain?"

"There are better things in this world than chasing a title."

"Would you call it just a title, or a title with *meaning*?" I question him, watching as he shakes his head. "For example; we have a King and a Queen in chess, and then we have all the other subjects. Each of them have a title and that title has meaning to it. Would you say that being the captain of the track team holds little to no importance to you?"

He grabs a hold of the King, and lifts it up to his eye. "I'm no King, Leon. I'm a pawn, ready to do the King's bidding."

"You may not be a King," I murmur, reaching over the table to hold his hand. "But with that pawn, you can be anything you want to be, only if you reach for it."

Nathan's gaze lands on our hands, forcing me to retract. He quickly grabs my hand again, this time, intertwining our fingers over the table.

"Maybe one day."

"You know, Nathan, you sound like you don't want to be a track star."

Nathan stares at me for a while, before letting go of my hand. "Can you keep a secret, Lee?"

I nod.

"I love being an athlete, I really do, but sometimes it just takes a lot of my mental and physical health. It's like I'm training to be the next Usain Bolt or something, and that's not what I want."

"If you don't want this anymore, then why can't you leave? You're entirely capable of it."

"I love running—"

"From your feelings or from life?" I accidentally blurt out loud, the heat to my cheeks climbing up quickly. However, Nathan's look after the words slip my mouth tell me everything I need to know.

There's something more to the problem than what he's letting on.

"Leon?"

"Yes?"

He looks conflicted. "What are you talking about?"

"I was...I was just asking. I'm sorry if I overstepped. I shouldn't have...Jesus, I'm so sorry."

Nathan's eyes widen a bit, before going back to normal, like something clicked in his head. "I'm running from both." He sighs, standing up. "I'll see you tomorrow."

I frown as he scurries out. Cece watches from a distance, and walks up to check on me while I continue to stare at the door, hoping that I didn't ruin any chances I may have had with him.

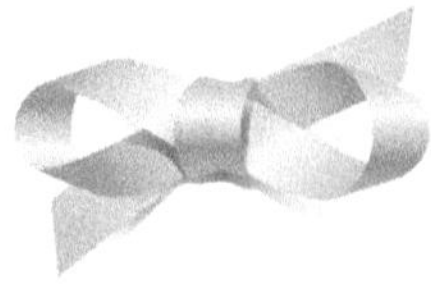

Chapter 11: Black Looks Good on You

Nathan left early to prepare for the house party he was hosting this weekend.

A party that I forgot he invited me to.

Once Cece finished fixing my collared black shirt, she turned to the mirror and began fixing her own hair. It's the first time I've ever seen her wear a pair of shorts and crop top, and if I'm being completely honest, she has a figure. The denim shorts hugged her waist perfectly, and the red crop top she paired it with brought out her defined collarbone.

I pick up the letter that I wrote for Nathan earlier during the day and contemplate on leaving it in his house. I didn't have enough time to give him the letter because everyone was just talking about his party, as well as Nathan actively avoiding me. At some point I thought I did something, but the realisation that he was probably just busy hit me harder than that morning coffee I forced down my throat this morning.

I'm going to make this real short. I didn't have the best day yesterday, but hopefully you'll make it better today.

So I've started this new thing called journalling. It's real cool, helps me deal with the stress and everything I experience. My mind can get a little too crowded for me, but with Journaling, I can at least put down some thoughts on paper.

When I'm done journalling, I usually get myself some food, then go to bed. But you don't want to hear about that.

I told you I'll make this short. I shouldn't even be breaking into your locker and placing this here. But it doesn't matter, you haven't reported me yet, have you?

Signing out,

J

"Derek's down, let's go." Cece flicks my forehead. She then grabs my paper. "Did you forget to send this one?"

"I got busy."

"Make sure you find a way to deliver it without Nathan seeing you," she advises. "Nathan makes sure to talk to everyone at his parties."

"Since when have you been to one of Nate's parties?"

"Since *forever*. You never go out, so that's probably the reason why you wouldn't know if I'm at a party of his or not," she explains. "In fact, I'm happy that this game has you getting out of your comfort zone, maybe I can finally introduce you to some li—"

"Let's go, Cece."

· · ❧ · ·

THE LENGTHS I GO TO for Nathan.

His parents' home is a stunning two storey house, a pool right outside, and a garage with a Range Rover inside. Inside, there's a spiral staircase, a bookcase next to the fireplace, and a large living room. The minimalistic interior design and shades of white and black makes the house astonishing. A glorious Australian home.

And right now, it's full of teenagers that reek of alcohol and cigar smoke.

The music's so loud I can swear my ears are going to burst as soon as I leave this place. Someone had handed me a red cup with some liquid inside it, but I refused to take it. Who knows what's inside it?

This is why I don't go to parties.

I lost Derek and Cecelia an hour ago, and in that hour was the time I consumed a bit of liquor. Derek gave me some, and just as much as I always have, I trusted him enough to not give me anything strong. He honoured that promise at least.

I walk up the spiral staircase and stare at the white door that has splatters of paint on it. I need somewhere quiet, and this seems to be the only place to get a bit of privacy and peace. I swing open the door to find Nathan upside down on the bed, a pack of licorice slipping out of his hand. On instinct, I drop the cup and help him up, the weight of his upper body forcing me to flex my upper arms in order to help him properly orient himself.

Once he's on the bed correctly, he squints his eyes at me. "Lee? I didn't think you'd show up."

The smell of liquor fans my nose. "Well I did," I answer, giving him a small smile.

He takes me by the hand and pokes my palm. "Your hands are soft," he says, then he looks up at me. "You look good."

I feel the heat rush up to my cheeks again. "Thank you, Nate."

His blue eyes scan my brown ones. "This is the first time I've seen you like this."

I frown, not sure of where this is headed. "Like what?"

"Like...*this.*" He pulls me closer to him a bit, and caresses my cheek. "This is the first time I've seen you in this light."

Flustered, I back away a little. He stands up and follows me, his hands gently holding me in place. "Nathan...you're drunk." I close my eyes briefly.

"I know what I feel, Leon," he whispers. "I know what I feel."

We stand in silence for a minute, the music finally no distraction to us. I wait for something...*anything*, while he continues to stare at me like I'm the only person in the world that can make him feel some sort of way. Hold on...*I make Nathaniel Daniels feel some type of way.*

Me. Leon.

"You're drunk," I repeat. As much as this moment means everything to me, I can't tell if he's acting off of his drunk feelings or if he's actually serious, and I'm not willing to take the risk. "Don't do this."

There we go, Leon. Do the right thing.

"Why?"

"Because...because you won't remember any of it in the morning."

It's true. He won't remember kissing a guy, he won't even remember I was here at his party. Maybe that would be for the best anyway; I can't leave him feeling like he made the biggest mistake in the world.

"Then...then that's a risk I'm willing to take." He smiles, and before I can reply, his lips press onto mine softly. Nathan kissed me.

Holy shit, Nathaniel Daniels kissed me.

And he isn't stopping. *Nathan is not stopping.*

I don't think I want him to stop anyway.

Nathan stops, and shakes his head. "I'm sorry, is this okay? Like...are *you* okay with doing this?"

I don't hesitate in my answer. "Yes, Nathan, it's okay."

He chuckles to himself. "Okay."

And our lips connect again

I don't know what I thought this moment would feel like. Heck, I wasn't even sure if I'd ever get to this moment I'm my life. But...it's nice. He's everything everyone has ever said about him; gentle and soft. He doesn't kiss with any urgency, it's as if he wants to savour this moment as much as I am, and his hands are in one place at a time; first my neck, then my hair. I don't even know what I'm doing; my hands are everywhere, struggling to find one position till he stops the kiss and takes my hands, wrapping them around his neck as he smiles. That's when I notice the height difference between me and him; how he's slightly taller than me and how he seems to have more balance than I do right now.

Who am I kidding? He's Nathan, of course he does.

We start kissing again, and this time, his hands are on my waist as he guides us closer to the wall. He pulls away and locks the door, checking to make sure it really is secure. Once he's done, he comes back for another kiss, his attention now on my neck as I whimper, trying not to make a sound when he bites down on the nape of my neck.

"It's okay, we're home," he reassures me. "It doesn't matter."

Something about the way he says the word *home* makes my heart flutter. I melt into the kiss, the thoughts of whether he will remember this or not leaving my mind. One thing is for sure though;

I'll remember. And even if this may be the closest I'll ever get to him, I'll be able to die happy knowing that Nathaniel kissed me.

"I'm home," I whisper, and he stops kissing me, just for a moment.

"You are." He kisses me on the cheek one last time before pulling away. "This is home."

Chapter 12: Hangovers and The 2 Letters

We're home.

    I wake up with a grin on my face and half a headache due to last night's events. I don't know about you, but I can die happily knowing that at some point, Nathaniel Daniels locked lips with *me*.

Nate's in bed with me, his head covered by a pillow and his soft snores filling the air. I try my best to get out of bed without waking him, but he snorts and twists, shaking the pillow off his head to peek at me. I wave at him, waiting for him to say something before I do.

"You stayed the night." He sounds more relieved than confused.

"I did...do you remember anything from last night?"

Nathan sits up and analyses me, cocking his head to the side. Fortunately, he shakes his head. "Vaguely."

Vaguely. "Well, that's fine. I'm going to head out now, I'm sure you'd like some alone time."

"Why? You haven't had breakfast yet," Nathan says, removing his shirt to reveal his six pack. "Wouldn't be fair for you to leave without eating."

"I shouldn't even be here," I mutter.

"But you are, therefore you're my guest." He gets up and fixes his hair a bit. "I'm going to go start up breakfast. Are you coming?"

Remembering that I had two more letters to write for the weekend, I grin, shaking my head. "I'll catch up with you, I need to take a shower."

Nathan chuckles. "Okay. Eggs and bacon?"

"Lovely."

With that, he leaves the room. Once the door shuts, I begin to scramble for a pen and paper. I still have 16 days left to do this, and I won't stop writing just because of a drunk kiss that he has no recollection of. He may have thought I was a girl or something.

Either way, Nate kissed me, and I'm taking this to the grave.

Well, you definitely know how to throw a party.

By the way, your party is trending already. I've seen photos and videos everywhere. Hopefully, you'll have a positive reaction when I finally reveal who I am.

Anyways, I hid this letter with both of my letters because I had no way of delivering these letters during the weekend.I hope you have a great weekend, and don't worry, my next letters are gonna come really soon.

Signing out,

J

Hiding the note in his backpack, I tear another piece of paper and take a second to think about what to write next.

Like I said, because it's a weekend, it's kind of hard for me to deliver these letters now.

Anyways, I hope you had a great party and weekend, don't forget to text everyone who attended. That's if you can, of course. There were a lot of people there anyway. Also, I might be close to selling myself out, but who cares? Certainly not me.

I have been meaning to give you clues of who I am. Maybe I will on Monday.

Signing out,

J.

"Lee, breakfast!"

I pack the letter away in his notebook this time, putting the notebook back in his bag. "Coming!"

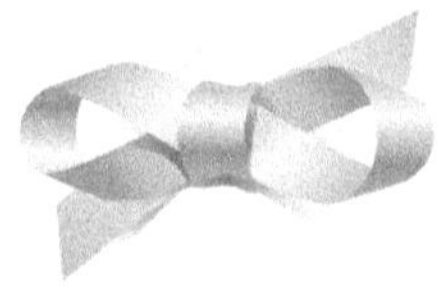

Chapter 13: Letter Number 7

Isn't it funny how we all fall in love at the wrong times?

I think it's safe to say that I might have fallen in love with you. There, I said it.

I haven't been that upfront with my feelings for you, and I probably won't be anyway.

But I felt that I needed to share this with you. I really like you, Nathan. Like actually like you, it's weird to me.

Sometimes it's hard to express my feelings. My mind gets clouded and I freeze everytime I try to talk to you about how I feel. But with writing, it just feels safer and much easier to communicate with you. I'm not scared of you at all, but I'm scared of how you'll react when you figure out who it really is. I don't want you to fall in love with the illusion of me, but with where I'm headed, that just might be the case.

I bet you can't count how many times I said the word "like" in this letter. It would be fun if you did.

It's really different for me. Like this is something real. And you won't know who I am. At least not yet.

You haven't replied to my other letters, that's okay. I never was expecting a reply from you anyways. But here we are, you replying to me without replying to me. Get it?

You probably don't.

Anyways, I hope you have a great day today. I'll just be here, watching you from a distance.

Signing out,

J.

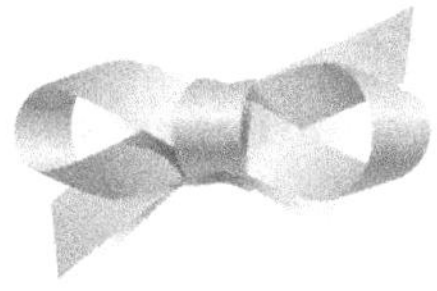

Chapter 14: Letter Number 8

I've been watching way too much Lion King lately.

I really feel connected to Disney movies. It's just so fun to watch, and they always teach you these lessons that you probably won't learn until you're older.

That's if you already learnt them.

Anyways, where was I? Oh that's right, my love for Disney movies.

I have no idea if you'd agree with me, but I actually love the element of getting a bit of magic with life lessons involved. Like Moana, teaching us about following the ocean and where it leads us(I'm joking, that's not the actual lesson) and other stuff like that.

I like that magical element it adds to our ordinary lives.

I mean, look at me, some human writing letters to a boy that I like instead of going to confront him about my feelings. That's sad, isn't it?

I'm not the best at courting men. Or women. Or anyone in general.

Moving on, The Lion King has me emotional nowadays. I mean, I know it's for the plot but SCAR IS A BITCH!

If you really wanted the kingdom from your brother, just go fight him and get it, instead of murdering him and blaming the poor death on Simba.

I stan Simba, except for the fact that he and Nala are practicing incest in front of my eyes. SWEET HOME ALABAMA.

Besides the fact I hate Scar, Simba is just amazing, dude. I mean, you gotta give it to him, he does take his rightful place-

You know what, I should stop rambling.

I would love to explain more if you wanted me to, but right now, I'm gonna go and sleep.

Signing out,

J.

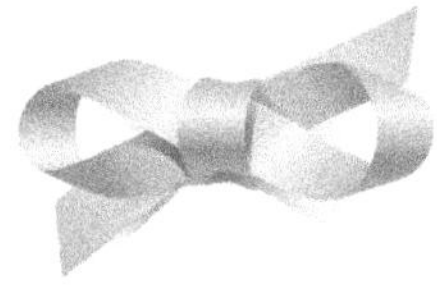

Chapter 15: Another Reply

Lion King was my movie growing up. It's still my comfort movie to this day actually.

Sorry I haven't been replying. Life has been getting a little hectic and I've been busy, but I promise you, I'm receiving these letters. And I love them, just like how I might be an idiot falling for someone through paper. Is this how they do online dating nowadays? What can I call this? Paper dating?

Sorry, I'm trying to copy your humour. How was I for my first go?

Anyways, I understand the feeling of not being able to confront your feelings, trust me, I've been there before. Multiple times. Believe it or not, the guy that everyone wants at school isn't the guy that has gotten who HE wants. Odd, right? I feel like people give me too much power, and they only give me that power because of how I look. It's funny to me, because I literally look like every other average Joe; just a kid with blonde hair and blue eyes. What should I do to make myself look...less noticeable? Should I get contacts?

Okay...maybe not the best idea.

As I write to you, I either gain or lose brain cells along the way. Is that a good or a bad thing? I think it's a good thing actually. You seem really smart, I need the brain cells.

Let me keep this short and cute. I can't wait to meet you. Maybe we'll be able to watch The Lion King together.

Nathaniel♡

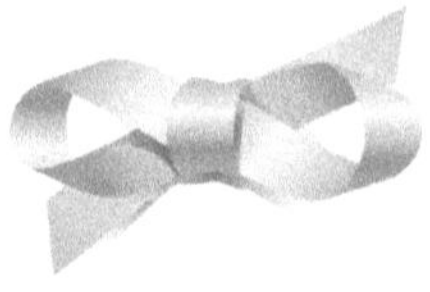

Chapter 16: Letter Number 9

I have come to the conclusion that I am a huge wimp.

And you have to know this, Nathaniel.

So, when I was writing my economics test, my good old friend passed me a note. She said I should meet her and we'd go skinny dipping together as a challenge.

I'm totally not going skinny dipping later.

I'm not as adventurous as you are, but I could try out new things if you had asked me. I'm always up for new things. Always.

Anyways.

You replied to me the last time, and I realise I haven't done the best job in courting you. I think I'll try better but when I do, don't answer the cheesy notes.

Unless you have something cheesier to reply with.

So, let me start courting you now.

Remember when I told you about the garden? My favourite garden?

Last night I went there(my parents thought I was coming from my friend's house) and I watched the night sky shine with stars.

It was stunning. I was in complete awe and suddenly felt that it wasn't right for me to be there alone.

So I imagined you next to me. Stupid, I know.

It was just amazing. I wanted to tell you who I am, but then another thought crossed my mind.

You might not accept me for who I am.

I finally got up after a good hour of staring at the sky, and realised that when the world is quiet, that's when your thoughts roar the most. It's when you can choose to be lost in your own world, so in that moment, I decided to get lost in the Garden of Eden.

And in that garden, I couldn't stop thinking about you.

Signing out,

J

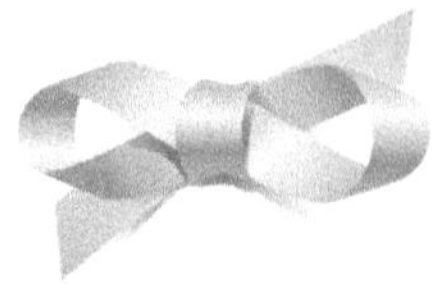

Chapter 17: The Garden Of...

As someone who has never been famous or popular, when Derek called me to watch him practice, I couldn't help but wonder; what is he up to now?

I arrive and sit on the bleachers, shocked to see Cecelia there already. She waves at me, the wind blowing in her now short brown hair.

"I still hate the fact that you cut your hair," I murmur.

"Change is good," she defends. "Change is necessary."

"Not always." I look at the field, and stand when a fight breaks out between Matthew and Nathan, who are quickly separated by Derek and the rest of the team. Cecelia and I exchange a glance before rushing onto the field.

"A fucking title is going to destroy our bond?! Fuck you, Matt—get the fuck off me!"

Nathan shoves Derek off of him, while Derek stumbles back, a look of disbelief engraved on his face. Cecelia goes to Derek and checks on him while I steadily approach Nathan, who backs away briefly, before taking me by the hand.

"Leon," I hear Derek call out. "Come back here, now."

I stare at Nathan, whose rage slowly disappearing as he looks at me. Against my better judgement, my hand remains connected to his, the yelling around us getting louder.

"Fucking faggots!" Matthew shouts, picking up a rock and attempting to throw it at Nathan, being stopped by Derek and the rest.

I hold my eye contact with Nathan, watching as he goes from calm to angry...and possibly embarrassed. His grip on my hand tightens, and he tries to pull me away from the scene when Derek latches onto my other hand, putting me in between them.

"Leon, I want to explain," Derek says. "Don't go. Not now."

"Lee," Nathan pitches in. "I'm fine with whatever decision you make. Stay or go, I won't force you. *Ever.*"

Conflicted, I sigh, letting go of both their hands. I look at Cece, who nods at me. She then mouths the word 'go' while latching onto Derek's arm.

"Go on Leon. Go on like the little boy that you are," Matt taunts. "Bet Nathan wants to take you behind the bleachers and f—"

"Take him to the locker room or something!" Derek snaps while the boys follow his request blindly, Matt cackling as he goes to the locker room.

I still don't understand what's happening, but from Matt's actions, I have a feeling. My stomach drops as if I'm the one that has been called a slur, so I can only imagine how Nathan is feeling right now. Derek also seems to be hiding something, and as he glances at me with a worried look on his face, I know he's involved indirectly.

And because of this, I'm taking Nathan's hand.

Derek shakes his head. "I see how it is." He then yanks his arm from Cecelia's death grip and walks off the field, grabbing his bag off the bleachers.

Nathan doesn't smile, he doesn't say a word. He acknowledges my choice by nodding, and we begin to walk out together, leaving Cece and the field behind.

.. ❧ ..

He took me to the garden.

I'm still in shock at this decision, but I need things to be explained, so I guess I can trust him with his destination choices. I wouldn't have trusted anyone to take me to the garden on a school day, *especially* when we're supposed to be at school at the moment. But I guess this is what Nathan does; he leaves the school whenever he wants to.

He will only subject me to this behaviour once, and never again. I'm Dominican.

Sitting down on the grass, I wait for him to explain, but when he doesn't say anything, I decide to break the ice.

"I didn't think you'd bring me here," I say, staring at his side profile.

"You told me that this was your safe space," he answers.

"And you remembered?"

"How could I not?" He then looks at me. "It's my safe space too. I wish I could have known about it sooner. Everything here is so peaceful, so calm. When I'm here, everything just leaves my mind. I'm at peace, and right now, I just want to be at peace."

"Peace is nice," I add. "Peace is good."

"The idea of escaping reality for a moment is why I always come here when things get rough," he explains. "The real world sucks sometimes, it's nice to forget after a while."

"How often do you come here?" I ask him.

"Everyday," he whispers. "I come here everyday."

Everyday.

There's silence between us as we look at the sun, watching it set. Perhaps the chance to escape reality, the perils of this world, and the terrors of the dark, are revived at the sight of the Garden for him. I know that's the case for me, because when I'm here, I have the chance to forget. To leave the timid, overshadowed Leon behind, and be...just Leon.

When I'm here, I'm only Leon.

"What happened, Nathan?" I finally ask.

He chuckles softly, picking at a tulip. "You know, I remember promising my mom I'd live under the radar because of my reputation. She told me if anyone knew, they'd try to use that as leverage and try to steal opportunities away from me. I should've known better, actually no, I should've hid it better. I thought no one would ever notice it."

"Notice what exactly?"

Nathan smiles bitterly. "I'm bi, Leon."

My anxiety turned into happiness for a brief moment, but I proceed to respond. "Okay?"

Nathan gulps. "Matthew and Derek found out. I guess I was acting extra suspicious lately, but they found out...and Coach Jameson has history of being homophobic, so he kicked me off the team without a proper reason. So...yeah, that's my life right now."

"Derek?" I ask. "I understand Matt but...*Derek?*"

"He was the one that found out and 'accidentally' told Matt. I don't know how it happened, but he fucked me over with that one. You need better friends."

"I don't think he meant to say it," I defend Derek even though my disappointment is evident. "Maybe it slipped out."

"Even if he did, it's none of his business, is it?"

"Nate, I understand you're upset but...I don't think Derek wanted this to happen. I don't know how everything went down but I'm sure he didn't intentionally out you."

"That's fine, I knew it would come out anyway," he mutters, hugging his knees. "I just wanted to come out on my terms, not come out because of an idiot that just wants the spot of a stupid high-school team."

"What if that's not the reason?"

"I won't look for the reason." He rocks himself lightly. "There is no reason."

Unsure of how to help him, I move closer to him and rub his back as he rocks himself. I haven't come out to the public yet, but the pain of having someone out you is overbearing, even if it doesn't seem as big of a deal to them. It's your choice. Everything you do on this planet should be *your* choice, and no one else's.

"You're not alone," I whisper. "I know how you feel."

"What?"

"I...like guys, Nate," I admit, smiling a bit when he stops rocking himself. "I'm gay."

He stops hugging his knees and looks at me. "So...you're just like me?"

My smile grows wider. "Yes, Nathan. I'm just like you. I'm just like every other person on this planet, and you want to know how?"

"How?"

"Because no one is really different from each other anyway. Deep down, we're all the same. Some may have better clothes or are privileged, but we're all the same inside. So yes, I'm just like you." I nod. "You know, I never really came out to anyone but Derek and Cecelia."

"You're lying."

"I'm not." I look at the sky. "I don't know if I want to come out to anyone else. I mean, I like the idea of people knowing, but I just don't want to get bullied by the team more than I already have."

"You never will," Nathan says. "I'm here now."

"What does that change?"

"Everything," he elaborates. "I've been defending you, and I'll continue to do it."

Bewildered, I squint my eyes and scoot away from him a bit. "What do you mean you've been defending me?"

Nathan sighs deeply. "I got a lot of shit from hanging out with you. I still do." He shakes his head in disappointment. "It wasn't just Matt and Thomas, but it was basically the whole team. Derek and I were always at your defence, and when they started suspecting that you were gay, things only got worse for Derek and I because we are your friends. But I'm not going to stop though. I'm going to continue to defend you."

The thoughts are coming back. "I don't think I'm supposed to be here with you right now," I admit, lowering my head. "I think you should go home."

Two fingers press under my chin, lifting my head up gently. His blue eyes scan my brown ones, trying to find any means of hesitation.

"Don't go."

He maintains eye contact as I gulp. "It's getting late."

"You are my home, Leon." He whispers.

My eyes widen as I remember when he used that phrase before. He last used it when he was drunk. When he kissed me.

When he kissed me.

"You weren't flat out drunk, were you?" I utter.

Confused, he cocks his head. "What are you talking about?"

"Oh, nevermind." I quickly take back. Reaching for the letter of the day in my pocket, I stop the urge to give him directly and reveal myself. Instead, when he turns to gaze at the sun, I whip the letter out and throw it behind him, somewhere discreet. He turns to check on me, and I smile, moving a little closer to him. "So what are you going to do about the issue?"

"What can I do about it? Matt's got what he wanted, right? No one is going to try and take the position he wants so badly now, he made sure of it," Nate admits.

"That's not the Nathan I know."

"The Nathan you know would fight, right? But right now I feel so defeated, Leon. I don't think I can fight this battle. The coach is known for being homophobic, it's a fight I won't win."

I hum, then look behind me. "Look, someone left something here."

Nathan turns his back and chuckles. He reaches over to grab the letter, and waves it in my face. "Of course this has to come to me now. J has a way of reaching me, huh?"

I rub the back of my neck nervously. "Yeah, your secret admirer is a genius."

Nathan doesn't respond as he opens the letter. "Life may be harder but you know what else is? School. Studying sucks but I need an education. You know what I also need? Is for you to trust and believe that I'll tell you who I am soon. I hope your day is as beautiful as you, Nate. Signing out, J."

"So that's J." I wriggle my eyebrows as he punches my shoulder lightly.

"Don't do that, Lee. It's a cute letter." He pouts, laying on his back and gazing at the sky.

I do the same, watching the clouds pass us by slowly. "It is."

"I can't wait till the reveal," Nathan says. "I have something special for them."

My eyes widen for a brief second. "What?"

"A magician never reveals his secrets." He chuckles. "But this made my day a little better. The person next to me made sure to stick beside me today, and that changed my entire mood. Thank you."

I grin. "You're welcome."

I'm not going to stop here. Nathan said he's not going to fight Coach Jameson and Matt, so I will. I'll fight for him because I want to. And I'll fight for him because it's only right. We should be allowed to love whoever we want and not be discriminated for it, no matter what.

And if it means I have to go through my school bully and the coach, then so be it.

"You're welcome," I repeat, closing my eyes.

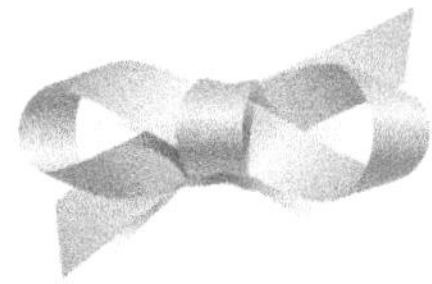

Chapter 18: Don't Run From Your Fears

It took me one night to map out how I'd do this right. After a long chain of events including writing Nate's letter *and* leaving a rose petal on it for the flair, I've come up with a simple plan to help Nathan get his spot and respect back.

Step 1: walk into the homeroom class and pray that Matt is alone and isn't with his group of jocks.

Step 2: confront him peacefully about Nathan

Step 3: pray I don't get punched in the face and try to confront the coach.

That's simple enough, right?

I walk into the class without Cecelia or Derek for the first time. Cece and I talked about what happened over the phone, but we both haven't responded to Derek. Derek's been blowing up my phone since last night, and honestly, I'm conflicted. I want to know why he did this, and why he didn't tell me about everything going on in the team. I get that I'm not an official team player, but if the conversation is about me, come to me as well, I can handle it...sometimes.

But Derek is a good friend for sticking up for me. Not a lot would do that.

I glance at every 10th grader in their free period, making eye contact with Derek briefly. My heart begins to beat faster as I see Matthew, and I begin to approach him holding onto my bag tightly. He looks up at me as I stand in front of his desk. Kicking his feet off the desk, he stands up, towering me a bit.

"And to what do I owe the pleasure of the chess captain looking at me?" He smirks.

"I...I want you to leave Nathan alone," I say.

Bewilderment turns into disbelief as he places a hand against his ear. "Excuse me? I didn't hear you." His friends laugh.

Gaining the confidence I need, I repeat my statement. "I want you to leave Nathan alone. It wasn't your place to reveal anything about him, and I won't stand for you bullying him, Derek or me. Not as long as I'm alive."

"Hold on, is anyone seeing this or am I hallucinating? Leon James, telling me to leave Nathan alone?" He mocks. "Is he your boyfriend now?"

"Hey man, stop that." Derek stands up.

"Or maybe Leon wants to be in the spotlight for once, huh?" Matt then claps his hands, grabbing everyone's attention while I begin to hyperventilate. "Listen up, I have something to say."

My breathing starts to become shallow as Matt grabs my arm and brings me to the front of the class. "Leon here is a special kid. You see, he and I go *way* back. I thought he was weak at some point, but you know what? Even the weakest of people have their time to shine. So Leon here is going to be the first openly *gay*—"

Nathan rushes out of his seat, with Derek following closely behind him. Derek punches Matt and Nathan pulls me out of the chaos, closing the door behind him.

I continue to hyperventilate as he pulls me into am empty classroom and shuts the door. I fall to my knees and scrunch up my blue shirt, the pain in my chest only increasing.

Nathan suddenly cups my cheeks together as he kneels down. "Lee, listen. It's okay, alright? Take deep breaths and let them out slowly. I'll help you, alright? Breathe in."

He releases me and I continue to look at him, taking a deep breath.

"Breathe out slowly," he says, nodding as a way to encourage me. "I'm not going anywhere, alright? I'm here."

I do it, my eyes focused on him.

"Now let's count to 5, okay?" He whispers, rubbing my arm up and down gently.

"One..." I take another deep breath and let it out again. Nathan smiles as we continue, my body slowly relaxing. "Two..." *Think of the clouds, Leon. The clouds.* "Three." I close my eyes and hang onto Nathan, gripping his arms. "Four." I completely relax, the pain in my body from the energy I used evident. "Five."

I hug Nate tightly, melting into his arms as he rubs my back. "I told you I'm not going anywhere."

"Thank you," I croak out. "Thank you."

It takes Nathan a couple of seconds to respond. "No, thank you. For standing up for me...I didn't think anyone would."

"Someone has to," I whisper in his ear while my breathing regulates. "And I made that decision."

"You made the choice," Nathan murmurs. "You fought for me."

I let go of him, smiling. "I fought for you because you fought for me."

We gaze at each other, and he smiles at me. "My sister has panic attacks sometimes. That's why when I noticed the signs I intervened."

"Usually Derek or Cece would've done something," I reply. "But I guess they had no business being there for me this time."

"Are Derek and Cece always there?"

"Yeah," I answer. "Ive always relied on them."

"Don't."

"What?" I croak.

"Leon, I don't want you to wait for someone to do something for you. I want you to stand on your own two feet, like you did today," he says. "Because I promise you, you are more than just the nerdy kid everyone paints you out to be."

I look down, but he tilts my head back up. "I'm not saying you shouldn't accept help every now and then, or that Derek and Cece should stop hanging around you. They're good friends, but I want you to find your identity outside them as well. I've seen you guys around, and I don't like how they have their own things going on, but the only thing you have going on is chess. Step out of their shadow and create your own name."

He was right. I do hide behind them. But not because I don't have an identity, but because it scares me to show everyone who I really am.

"Derek and Cece were the only ones that really ever listened to me," I admit. "I hid behind them because I don't know how to be accepted for who I truly am. I created a version that no one will notice, the one in the background; the guy behind Derek and Cece. I want to be accepted for who I am."

Nate pats my shoulder. "Then *be* who you are. People like to judge each other anyway."

"That's what I'm running away from."

"Someone once told me that running from our fears is cowardice because they'll catch up to us anyway," he quotes me. "We face them head on. Everyday, Lee, everyday. I faced mine, now it's time to face yours."

And with that, Nate walks away, leaving me in the class alone.

Chapter 19: Friends and Foes

Cece saved our usual table. The only difference is; there's no Derek.

Derek and Matt have allegedly been suspended for a couple of days, which makes sense. Plata High School takes its social issues seriously, and this is the other reason I want to report the Coach. If they took Matthew and Derek as seriously as they did, imagine how serious they'll take a homophobic coach kicking off his best athlete because of his sexual orientation.

I walk through the cafeteria, a couple of eyes on me. After the stunt I pulled homeroom yesterday definitely brought some attention to me, but for the first time, I can say I truly didn't care. If they talk about me, then they're talking about me. Nothing I can do to change or fix that.

But now onto the things I can actually change.

I sit down next to Cecelia, who is busy checking out someone at the other side of the cafeteria. I turn my head to look, and notice a dark skinned girl in the corner, sitting alone, with blue headphones in. She's laser focused on her book, and I turn to glance at Cece, who is still staring.

"Okay, what is going on here?"

"Didn't you hear?" She asks. "She's the new girl here. She allegedly came here from Perth, and doesn't really talk to people. Crazy, right?"

"Okay, understandable. But why are you staring at her?"

"Because I think..." Cece draws off. "I find her cute, okay?"

"You aren't with Derek anymore?"

"I didn't say that. I just find her cute, that's all. Is that a crime?" She shrugs.

"You didn't answer my question because I'm right, aren't I?"

"I mean, I was hoping I could talk to her—"

"Cece."

"Leon."

"Why did you and Derek break up?"

She sighs, putting the burger she was eating down. "We didn't see eye to eye on a couple of things."

"Like?"

"How can we handle your situation here? We tried coming up with a plan but...he didn't really agree with me." Cece looks away. "Everyone in our grade is talking about you, Derek, and Nathan. So Derek said we should ignore it, but I know how much you hate being in the spotlight and how much you–"

I close my eyes. "Derek's right."

"Pardon?"

I open them again to look at her, taking a deep breath. "Derek's right."

"How? That's not how we do things."

"Well, it is now." I firmly state. "Cecelia, you're right, I hate being the topic of conversation most of the time. I hate being at the forefront of gossip, I hate having people looking at me, and I hate being asked about shit that people shouldn't know or care about. But you know what I hate the most?"

"What?"

"Being overlooked, overshadowed, and having my battles always fought for me." I reach for Cecelia's hand. "Look, I appreciate the fact that you and Derek are always there to defend me and fight for me, but some battles just need to be fought alone. All I'd want from you two regarding this situation is patience, support, and love. I don't need you to go out of your way to fix my mess, I don't want to always hide behind my best friends when shit goes left. I have to go through this shit too, and that's exactly what I'm going to do. I hope you understand."

Cece's silent, her lips that were once pursed into a thin line slowly changing into a smile. "Wow, I guess you really are growing out of your shell." She squeezes my hand. "And we aren't here to stop that."

I smile back at her, then wink. "And I'm about to show you an example of that growth."

Cece's smile fades as I stand up, and walk towards the girl. I carefully think of what I'm about to say to her as I get closer to her table. Once I'm there, I tap the table to get her attention, which works like a charm. She removes her headphones and puts her book down, looking up at me with a fierce gaze. I return her glare with a warm smile.

"Hey."

"Is there something you need?" she immediately asks. "If this is your table, I can get up and go. I was told that no one–"

"Relax." I whistle. "I just wanted to invite you to come sit with us. My name is Leon, and I think we'd be great friends in the future. That's if you want to come over?" I politely ask her.

She thinks it over for a couple of seconds, before packing her bag and getting up. We walk back to our table, and she takes a seat next to me, a smile on her face. Cecelia stops eating and nods at her, looking nervous.

"Cece, this is..."

"Yvonne," she says. "I forgot to tell you my name, my bad."

"That's fine. Yvonne, this is Cecelia. Cecelia, this is Yvonne."

Cece harbours a nervous smile. "I'm Cece."

"Nice to meet you, Cece. And of course, it's nice to meet you, Leon," she murmurs. "I'm sorry for how I treated you at first. I still haven't fully processed the fact that I'm here and not in Perth, you know? I left a lot behind."

"I'm sure you did, but guess what? You're here now, at Plata, home of the panthers. You'll be safe here, especially with us. Right, Cecelia?"

Cecilia looks up from her lunchbox. "Absolutely."

Yvonne chuckles. "You know, you're way nicer than I thought you would be. A lot of people have been talking about you and Nathan or something. Like, you're a thing and because of that, he got kicked off the track team. Is it true?"

"We aren't a thing," I mumble. "But he did get kicked off the track team. I'll find a way to get him back though."

"How?"

"That's something that you won't have to worry about. Just know he'll be back there soon."

I'll make sure of it.

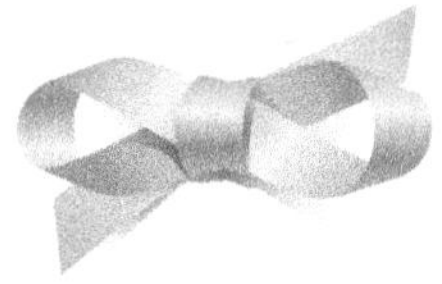

Chapter 20: Letter Number 11

Thank God you got my last letter. That was so hard to deliver considering I didn't have any tape or didn't hide it as well as I usually do. But hey, you got it, that's all that matters.

I think it's time that I reveal something that you probably know already. Yes, I go to Plata High School. And yes, I am in the tenth grade.

That's all I'm revealing.

Now why did I reveal this information when I've been vague about it in the past? Well, it's because I was there in the homeroom class the day you, Derek, and Matt got suspended. I was there, and I saw how you defended Leon. It showed me how selfless you are sometimes, and I admire that about you. You put others first, and one day, someone is going to put you first.

And I'm sure that day is close.

About the rumours going on that you and Leon may have something going on, don't even worry about it. Do whatever suits you better; you can deny them, or you can ignore them. This won't change the format of my letters to you or the tone, it'll only make my flirting game a little stronger. Why? Because the imaginary competition is what keeps me going.

I also wanted to give you some encouragement because I'm sure you're feeling a bit low. Do not care about what those people think of you, whether they're on the team or if they're the quiet kid in class going on with your story and how you are as a person. People talk and I know that, but sometimes you just have to keep going in order to live the life that you want to live. A happy life isn't a life without drama, issues, sadness or tears, it's a life that has overcome all of that and said fuck it, I'm going to live and I'm going to love it. So fuck the drama, fuck the homophobes, fuck the rumours and fuck that damn coach, live in your truth, and live it PROUDLY.

That's what I want you to do, that's what I KNOW you will do. And know that I'm standing behind you, every step of the way. Signing out,

J.

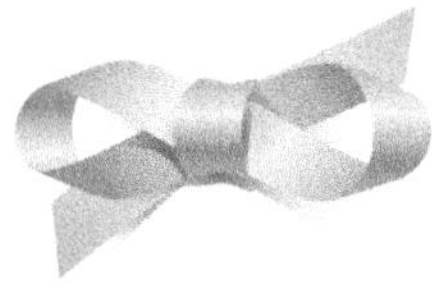

Chapter 21: Letter Number 12

Okay, I may be a bit of an idiot.

So remember in my last letter when I said that you should stand in your truth and be yourself? Yeah, when I was writing this letter I realised that I wasn't just giving you advice, I was giving myself advice too. In a way, by hiding behind these letters I'm not being myself. I'm not being open with you, and I am certainly not standing in my truth.

I hide behind these letters because a part of me is scared. Scared that you won't love me for me, and that when I reveal myself, you won't be happy with who's looking back at you. I like you a lot, Nathan, and I don't want you to fall in love with a fabricated version of me. This doesn't mean I will stop writing to you, please don't take the letter that way.

Do I enjoy writing these letters to you? Of course. But will you fall for the ink on the paper, or will you fall for the person holding the pen?

Just some thoughts. Sorry that this letter doesn't have much. I just wanted to put it out there.

Signing out,

J.

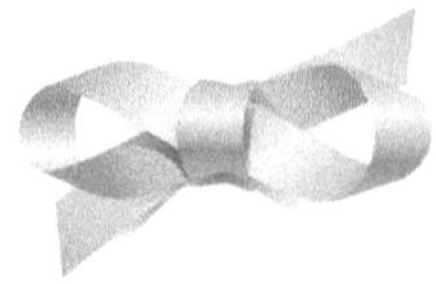

Chapter 22: The Person

I believe I'm falling for the person holding the pen.

While I do believe in people being open enough to talk to me because of how open I am, the letters were an interesting approach. Which is why I'm responding to them, you know. I could've ignored you, reported you to the principal, or worse, try to find you and murder you, allegedly.

ALLEGEDLY.

But yeah, I'm falling for the person, not the ink. I chose the person, not the ink. And I want the person to know that I will always choose them, no matter the cost. I pride myself in protecting the people I care about, and you also happen to be a part of them, even though I allegedly don't know what you look like. Maybe I am getting delusional, protecting a person I have allegedly never met.

But I know I have met you. Probably more than once.

You are somewhere at school. I may have even bumped into you a couple of times, or said hello to you and kept it moving. I may have even given you a pen when you needed one. All I know is that you are out there, and when the time is right for me to see you, I will. This gives me hope, and this gives me encouragement.

Love,

Nathaniel.

Chapter 23: The Power of Threats

Yvonne fixes my hair while I check the time, waiting for the coach to be in his office.

Today is the day. Today, I will get Nathan back on the team.

"Okay." she whistles at me. "How are your curls better than mine? I spent all morning on my hair."

"You know your hair is better than Leon's," Cece compliments her, trying her best to not touch her hair as she points at her afro puff. "Imagine if you had done two puffs. You'd look even prettier."

"Girl, I'd look like a fucking mouse."

"It's the Mickey Mouse Clubhouse!" Cece sings, while Yvonne ruffles Cecelia's hair a bit.

"Wish me luck ladies," I interrupt them, pressing the record button on my phone and hiding it deep in my pocket. "He should be in now. It's right after lunch."

"Okay, good luck—" Cecelia stops, watching as Derek walks over to us.

Derek hasn't spoken to me since the incident, and I'm not sure of what I want to say to him, or if I even have anything to say to him. So much has happened in less than 3 weeks, that I can't even form a coherent sentence to describe how I feel about everything.

"Where are you going?" he asks me. He then looks at Yvonne. "Hello."

"Derek," she responds.

Derek ignores her, and looks at me. "I need to talk to you."

Before I can say anything, Cece clears her throat. "Leon is going to go do something. If there's someone you might as well talk to, it can be me." she then nods at me. "Leo, go."

"I'll see you guys later."

I take long strides to the coach's office in order to avoid anyone stopping me while simultaneously ignoring the stares. I reach his door, and say a little prayer before knocking on the door. Hearing his voice, I enter, and close the door behind me.

"Leon! How are you, son?" He greets. "Take a seat."

"I'll stand, thank you." I clear my throat. "I would like to speak to you."

"Are you finally joining the track team? We have multiple spots open!"

I shake my head. "If you have multiple spots open, then why was Nathan, your best runner, kicked off the team?"

Coach Jameson's smile drops, and he sighs. "Leon, I train boys, alright? I try to train them into becoming men as well, because half of the boys on that team are on the rugby team. They are our future players, our future seniors, and because of that, they need to be strong and manly for all this. Nathan used to possess that, but because–"

"But because he's queer you decided it was time to let him go," I complete his sentence.

"Leon, I am not homophobic."

"Then why'd you really kick him off the team? Nathan has been on the team since we were freshmen, and he's always been a top runner, but suddenly your son tells you that he's gay and you decide that he's no longer good enough?"

"I—Leon, please leave my office." Coach Jameson shakes his head. "As much as I appreciate your concern about Nathan's departure, it has nothing to do with you."

"It has everything to do with me because you're letting your son dictate how you run the school team," I snap. "It has everything to do with me because the reason *your* son, Nathan and Derek got suspended for 2 days is because *your* son tried to belittle and bully us because Nathaniel is queer and I'm gay, Coach Jameson. So no, I'm not leaving this alone because it has everything to do with me and how your son has been treating us!"

The coach is silent for a moment, then he nods. "He has not influenced my decision."

"Okay, so how are you going to explain to Principal Carter why Nathan is no longer on the team at the next track event?" I cock my head to the side. "How are you going to answer him when he asks you why the one person that has brought us all the gold for the junior team is no longer there? How do you plan on explaining it? Or maybe—" I lean in a little closer to his desk. "Or maybe you wouldn't mind if I strolled into his office, and told him that

Coach Jameson kicked off our golden runner because he's queer and that's not masculine anymore?"

Coach Jameson remains silent.

"Nathan needs to be on that team because without him, we're going to lose our track events. Your son isn't fast enough, for one, and you know the rest of the team can only do the medley runs, but suck at the sprints and hurdles. If anything, Nathan needs to be your future captain because he has technique and strategy. He can make your team of shitty athletes into stars. You know that and you hate it." I sneer, taking out my phone and ending the recording. "He's getting back on that team, Coach Jameson. Or this recording is going straight to Principal Carter, who happens to have a daughter here. And guess what? Her daughter has two dads, Coach Jameson. Principal Carter has a *husband,* so I wonder how he'll react when he finds out that a member of staff is being homophobic to one of the students."

I start walking back to the door before the coach calls my name.

"Call Nathaniel in," he mumbles. "Now."

I smile, and look back at the coach. "Yes sir."

I leave his office and start laughing quietly, my back against the lockers. Thank God everyone is in their club right now, otherwise I'd look like a maniac standing alone in the hallway, laughing to himself. I sit down, shaking my head at how confident I was in there. The coach was probably shitting his pants after I said I was recording.

"Lee?"

I look up to see Nathan extending a hand out to me. I take it, getting up as he gives me a hug, his lemon and honey dew scent greeting me once more.

"I haven't seen you in ages," he whispers while I shut my eyes. "I missed you."

He missed me.

There's no need to lie here. "I missed you too."

We separate, and Nathan grins at me. He then pulls out pink lemonade, and gives it to me. "I've been walking around the school like an idiot, just looking for Lee because this is his favourite."

"Thank you," I reply. "Coach Jameson is looking for you, he's in his office right now."

Nathan frowns. "What does he need me for? I thought I was off the team?"

You were. "I'm not sure, just go see him," I lie. "I'll talk to you later."

Nathan nods his head in agreement. "Okay, later."

As he walks into the coach's office, I put the drink in my bag, while simultaneously taking out the next letter heading over to his locker to deliver it.

Chapter 24: Letter Number 13

And that, ladies and gentleman, is how Nathan got his groove back.

Yes, I watched How Stella Got Her Groove Back. It's a good movie, okay? Stan Stella for clear skin, Nate.

Kidding, your skin is so smooth dude. Drop that skincare routine, I know that it's not just water and soap.

Anyways, it's good that you're finally back on the team. I am happy for you, Nate. That's all I've been hoping for when it comes to you; that you fulfil your dreams without assholes trying to take it away from you. You deserve to be on the team. You deserve to be captain. And I just know that you will be captain next year.

I also like how this indirectly made Matthew look like an idiot. He's literally a real life Scarface; trying to take things that don't belong to him by any means necessary. You took control of the situation, Nate, and I like it when you're in control...of your narrative, of course.

Anyways, hope you had a good day, and don't forget to watch a disney movie tonight.

Signing out,

J.

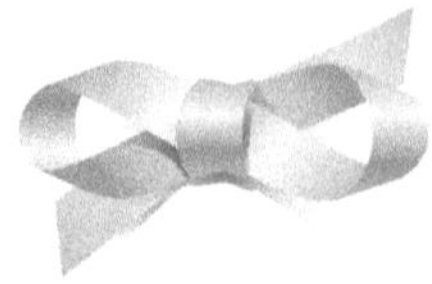

Chapter 25: Letter Number 14

Become the King to my Queen.

So I've been coming up with a few pickup lines that involve both chess and track. Let me tell you some.

Aren't you tired? Because you've been running around my mind all day. Terrible? I know.

So now I can safely say that I'm the worst at pickup lines, as stated in the example above. But perhaps I can do better in your bed.

But that's besides the point.

The point I am trying to make here is that you are admirable, and I would like to court you. Or fail to court you, same thing for me honestly. If that fails, I can make you laugh, because I'm sure you laughed right now, either at my horrible puns or at how smooth I am. Call me Michael Jackson cause my puns are smoother than his moonwalking. Get it?

Sometimes I wonder why I write these letters. I could literally walk up to you at school, at any given moment, and say it's me, splash you with confetti, then run away. That seems easier than this sometimes, you don't know how much effort I put into these letters and making sure you see them.

Maybe I'm a simp. But don't worry, just for you.

Signing out,

J.

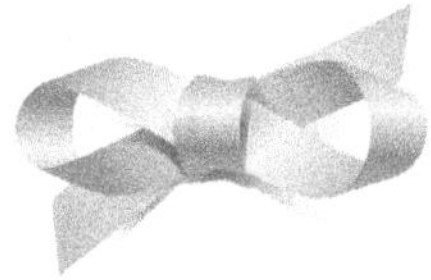

Chapter 26: Letter Number 15

Welcome to the next letter, the 2026 version of Troy Bolton.

There are so many nicknames I can give you: My Eden, Nate, King, so many. But I've already embarrassed myself enough. Anyway, let me talk about the real reason this letter is here.

I want to tell you about my first kiss.

It was messy, but in a good way. My thoughts tried to get the best of me and I was a bit tipsy but... I liked it. It was also with someone that I happened to like at the time, as well as him being tipsy as well. Sad that he doesn't remember any of it, it would've been fun if he remembered just a bit or even what I looked like, but he didn't. That's okay though, I'm sure the person receiving these letters will be insanely better than I've already heard that he is...

It's embarrassing to say that he was my first kiss. At 16, you'd think I've at least kissed one or two guys before, but things don't always work out for the person in the background, but I'm sure you already know that.

That's why, when the time is right, I will step out of the shadows, and reveal myself. The real me, the one you've been talking to through paper.

Signing out,

J.

Chapter 27: Derek

Okay, let's be real.

This past week has been messy. Very, very messy. From Nathan getting back on the team to Cecelia announcing her and Derek splitting, I can safely say that me sending letters to Nathaniel isn't the most batshit thing to ever happen to me.

I sit down next to Derek and watch the swimming team practice. Derek asked me to come see him, and since we never got the chance to talk during the week, he thought it would be best to talk now, considering none of us swim. Well, Cecelia does, but she's only trying out with no one focusing on me or him for once. Cecelia's on the swim team as well, and having us meet here as a trio again is one of the most sane things we've done in two weeks.

We watch Cecelia do the butterfly as she intentionally splashes water all over us, coming to the surface and blowing us a kiss. I shake my head as she goes back underwater, leaving us to continue training.

"It's been a while," says Derek as he fidgets and plays with a little rock in his hands.

"I truly wonder why," I mumble.

"Matthew quit the track team, if that makes you feel any better," he explains. "I don't know if Nate told you this, but I doubt he's going to say anything. We wanted to keep this a secret, or at least keep it under wraps for a little while. I just knew that I had to let you know."

I sigh, relief washing over me. "Thank God. I'm sure Nathan was really happy."

Derek nods. "Thanks to you."

My eyes widen and he looks at me, a small smile on his face.

"We all know you went to tell the coach off. Matt gave a speech about it anyway." He shrugs. "I'm impressed. When Cece told me that you're eager to be more confident and to stand by yourself at times, I didn't think you'd start by telling the coach to fuck off."

"I didn't tell him to fuck off," I whine.

"But you did stand up to him. It's rare for anyone to do that. Heck, even Cameron wouldn't do that and she's acting batshit crazy."

"I wonder what she's going to be like as a 12th grader when she's already acting bold in her freshman year," I add. "It's going to be one heck of a time."

"I wonder what we're going to be like as seniors." Derek shakes his head. "We're still in the first term of 10th grade."

"We got time." I pat his back. "We'll always have time."

Then there's silence.

I don't know how to address the elephant in the room. When Derek and I first set up this meeting, I was so confident that I'd ask about everything that's been happening behind the scenes. But now, as I am here, sitting beside him as time passes by, the fake confidence and messy pep talk that I gave myself before coming here slowly starts to manifest itself as the silence begins to eat me up from the inside.

Swallow me whole, dear silence, this is the only time I'll allow you to.

"Matthew overheard Nathan and I talking in the toilet," Derek suddenly says. "I never went up to Matt and told him that Nathan is gay. The story got warped by him and Thomas since that's all they can do; fuck shit up."

"What did you and Nathan talk about?" I ask, looking down.

"We talked about you. We talked about confusion, and we talked about confidence," he replies. "Nathan confided in me right after he confided in you."

Confused, I ask, "He talked about me?"

"Yeah, of course he did, Leon. Why wouldn't he?"

"Why?"

"He'd have to tell you that himself. I promised not to meddle in Nathan and Leon's story anymore. Cece forced me to."

"Hey!" Cece wipes her wet hand all over Derek's face. "Let Leon do his thing."

"He wouldn't have done his thing if it wasn't for me." Derek rolls his eyes.

"Okay cupid," she scoffs.

"I actually do need your help with a few things," I interrupt their bickering. "The both of you."

"With?"

"That's not important right now. What's important is me apologising to you for getting you suspended. I didn't mean to."

"Don't even worry about it, Leo. Best time of my life dude; I didn't have homework for three days!" Derek hollers.

"Thank you for reminding me about that; Jessica has your overdue homework," Cece chuckles as Derek pouts. "Bet you're going to enjoy all that work from Mr Lacoste. You know he wants his shit for half term."

"And he doesn't care about the zero on your report card," I add. "But Mama Adams will."

Derek groans. "Give me a damn break here. I just got back."

"From a one day suspension, yes. Not a jail sentence!"

"Shut up Cece!"

"Why are you on my ass when Leon hasn't even finished his bet?!" Derek points at me.

"How did I get into this?"

"Okay, let's get back to the topic!" Cece claps. "Derek, do you accept Leon's apology?"

"He never needed to apologise. It's just what friends do; friends protect each other." Derek shrugs.

"Alright, fair enough. Leon, do you accept Derek's request to renew the friendship?"

"Wait, we stopped being friends?" Derek and I exchange a confused look.

Cece pauses, then claps her hands. "Yay, friendship!"

She throws her damp body at us, the three of us losing balance and falling, laying flat on the concrete, laughing like hyenas. With the three of us back in each other's good graces, we can conquer anything.

Absolutely anything.

"So, what do you need help with?" Cece asks.

I look at the ceiling while smiling. "I thought you'd never ask."

Chapter 28: Letter Number 16

I want us to play a little game.

Well, if you're up for it, anyway. I thought that would be a better way for us to keep writing to each other. And another reason for this is because I don't want you to get tired of reading dumb letters from some anonymous person with barely any content or any reason as to why I'm sending the letters.

Wouldn't that be fun?

So, here's the game;

In future letters, I will add a clue inside the letter. It could be a word, a sentence, or even just one letter, but who am I to say what it is? That is for you to figure out. And knowing Nathan, he might just figure out what the goal of the game is.

Fun, right?

We can start the game with this letter. In this letter, there's a clue that I want you to find. I'm going to shut up now and let you figure it out, and hopefully, you will. If you manage to find all the clues, a reward will be given to you.

Good luck, Nathaniel!

Signing out,

J

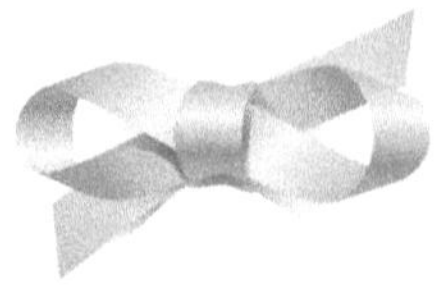

Chapter 29: Letter Number 17

Have you ever thought about going skydiving?

Just a random question, but guess what? I just put another clue in that sentence. I swear I'm too kind. I'm literally giving you hints for FREE.

Anyways, back to skydiving.

That's a big NO for me. And knowing you, you might just force me to go skydiving. That's if you ever figure out who I am. We both know that you will, but I'm just making myself clear because you may never see me. At least, in person. Why? Because I'm terrified.

There's a lot of things that I'm scared of actually, but we'll talk about that another time. Today, let's talk about my fear of heights.

I gave the example of skydiving. Being in the sky, letting go and jumping back to the fucking ground sounds easier said than done. You can lie to your friends and say you're going to go skydiving, but once you get in the air, you'll be begging for that pilot to land. I can't imagine being suspended in the air for a long period of time.

If you ever force me to go skydiving with you and you back out last minute, best believe I'm pushing you off that helicopter for even TRYING to get me out of my comfort zone.

Well, I'm already out of my comfort zone anyway, if you knew the amount of shit that I've been doing ever since these letters, you'd be surprised.

And a little terrified.

Good luck finding that clue, Nate. And no, it's not us going skydiving.

Signing out,

J.

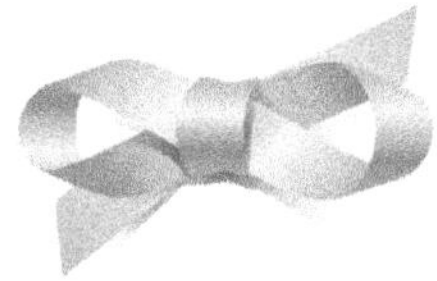

Chapter 30: Letter Number 18

Adored the song "Shower" by Becky G. This song gets me in a happy mood. It also manages to make me think about the type of love I'll never receive in this lifetime. The type of love that gets people talking, the type that makes life worth living, and the type that gives you a reason to keep going.

Perhaps you can show me that one day.

I really hope you can show me that one day.

If you haven't listened to the song, you should. I sound like a major Becky G stan right now, of which I am, but the song just makes me think of you now. I always see you at school, and on the days that I do get to talk to you, my entire world shifts. If I was sad, your presence makes me happy, if I was feeling worthless, your presence would be the one to encourage me to live life. That's all I've been trying to do for the past two weeks or so; live life.

And in a way, writing to you made me live a little.

Hope you found your next clue.

Signing out,

J.

Chapter 31: Letter Number 19

You will always be my Eden.

Before you think this is the last letter, it isn't. However, it is one of the last letters, Nathan, and before they end, I have a few things to get off my chest. A few things that I'm sure will either make you cringe or make you smile.

Hopefully I get the second reaction.

Have you ever watched the show Bridgerton? You know, the one where all those royal Bridgerton kids try to find love and mate?

Yeah, that one.

Let's talk about Kate and Anthony for a second. Did I love them? Yes. Did I root for them from the beginning? Absolutely. But do I think we were robbed of more scenes of the two?

YES. The answer will always be YES.

I'm just like Kate's little sister, Edwina. I love trying to fit in and try new things, but at the same time, I am Kate: I rather stick to what I know best. What I promised myself I'd do.

And sometimes I ask myself; what promise did I make to myself?

I promised that I wouldn't run from my fears anymore. And somewhere, somehow, you helped me face a few. Thank you for that.

You are the bane of my existence.

Signing out,

J.

Chapter 32: Letter Number 20

For the record, I suck at this game.

As the person that set it up, I'm disappointed in myself. I call the shots, yet I'm here failing to even get the clues out. I don't know how to write the clue into this letter. Or maybe I just did.

Gaslighting 101.

Fuck, I'm confusing myself. The goal is to confuse YOU, not confuse myself. I wish i could ask you for help but by the time I send this letter it'll be too late. Now, onto the topic of the day; my special secret.

Nathan, I am a Swiftie. Possibly, the first of my kind.

Well, that's not the real secret. In fact, let me talk about Miss Taylor. It's going to confuse you, but that's what these last letters are for; confusion.

My favourite song by Taylor is Daylight because again, this song reminds me of you. There are a few other songs that remind me of you, but I run to this song first because at times, I feel like I'm messing up my chances with you. I know that my thoughts may get the best of me sometimes...but when I play this song and think of you, I go to a different dimension. I'm at peace with myself, and I'm at peace with the world.

Reminds me of the duet by Flynn Rider and Rapunzel in Tangled. I know you watched that movie, and I know you ugly cried at the song and at the lanterns show. That's not the point though. From the song 'I See The Light, there's one line I particularly loved, and I'll finish off the letter with this line;

And at last I see the light.

Signing out,

J.

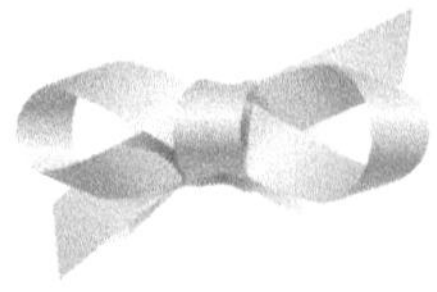

Chapter 33: Letter Number 21

The longest time, or should I say wait, has finally come to an end. This is the last letter.

The last letter you'll receive in your locker. The last letter that you'll receive anonymously. And the last letter you'll read before getting to see the face behind J.

Honestly, I've had fun writing these. And I've had fun talking to you through them. At some point, I would ask myself, 'Am I okay with him falling in love with a fabricated version of me? No. But what other choice do I have?' instilling so much fear in myself. I never thought I'd get this far with my letters thing, or that you'd read them, but here you are.

Here *we* are.

Nathaniel Daniels, meet me at the Garden on Friday after school. You know which garden.

I'll reveal everything to you there. This is my promise to you.

As the last letter you'll receive before my big reveal, I would like to say thank you for giving the letters a chance, and even reading them. Some of them were a bit cringey, but that's what I'm here for; if you're not laughing at my embarrassing letters, then you're most definitely laughing at my non-existent sense of humour and charm. What can I say? J has a few tricks up their sleeve, and J also happens to be very romantic.

You'll see on Friday.

It has been an absolute pleasure writing to you, Nathaniel Daniels. And I can't wait to see you on Friday.

Signing out,

J.

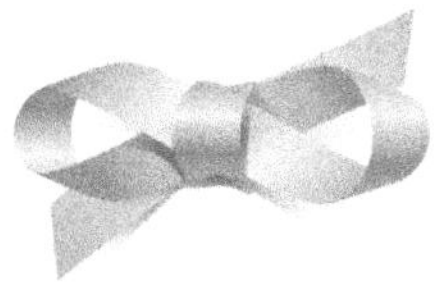

Chapter 34: The Last Letter.

"**G**osh, Cecelia, the banner isn't high enough! We want the banner to reach the fucking stars!" Yvonne scolds Cece, who almost loses her balance as Yvonne shakes the ladder.

"If you continue shaking that ladder we'll see who's going to be seeing stars in a minute!" Cece yells, forcing Yvonne to stop. Cece ties the string on the pole, and whistles. "Okay! Now, hold the ladder steady."

"That's what I've been doing."

"Yeah Cece," Derek fixes my collared shirt. "Yvonne won't drop you. You're a fragile egg in her eyes."

"Shut up Derek," they both say.

Today's the day.

Cece, Derek, Yvonne and I left school early to prepare the Garden for this. This was the only help I truly needed; man power. Four people working on one thing is easier than one person working on it. Besides, I needed to thank them for everything; especially Derek.

Derek whistles while holding the picnic basket. "Okay, what time is it?"

"Shit, it's almost 4!" Cecelia panics. "What time is he supposed to come?"

"Any minute now—"

"That's our cue then," Yvonne mumbles. "I'll see you guys on Monday. Cece—" she winks at Cecelia. "Text me."

Cece's mouth drops as Yvonne blows her a kiss and walks off. Derek and I exchange a look, and then stare at Cece.

"Cece?"

"I...have fun, Leon. I'm just going to..." She drawls off, then picks up her bag and runs out the garden, leaving me with Derek.

"She likes Yvonne, doesn't she?" I ask him.

"And it seems like Yvonne likes her too," he replies.

"Are you happy for them?"

"Of course I am," Derek says. "Cecelia's happiness is always on my mind. Besides, I think I'm going to ask Jessica out soon."

"Jessica? The redhead?"

"Yes, my sweet Merida," he coos. "Wish me luck."

"You don't need luck," I chuckle. "But if you need a bet, you know I'm down to give you one." I wink at him, then smile. "Thank you. I wouldn't have done all this if it wasn't for you."

Derek nods, then hands me the picnic basket. "I got you, Leo."

As soon as Derek reaches the entrance to the garden, Nathan enters the garden. They stop to acknowledge each other, with Derek giving Nathan a pat on the back.

The basket in my hands begins to shake as Nathan approaches me, his bag slung over his shoulder. His blonde hair looks golden in the wary afternoon sun, and the green track jacket threatens to escape his broad shoulders, Nathan finally taking it off and throwing it to the ground. He gets closer to me, and then looks into the basket, where his last letter rests on top of the snacks.

"J," he says softly. "I'm glad I was right."

"Was that obvious?" I chuckle nervously.

"Could be the fact that you and I did spend the night together. Or maybe the fact that these letters only began when you got a bet from Derek. And shout out to him, he's a good friend, by the way. I was wrong about him."

"Wait why are you—" The realisation settles in. "You told him about me."

"Because he knows you." Nathan opens his bag, and empties it, all the letters I wrote falling to the ground. "And I think I know you too."

I gape at the letters, shaking my head. "You...you kept them."

"Why wouldn't I?" Two fingers come under my chin, gently guiding my head so that I can look at him. "And I believe I have one last letter. May I have it? Or do you want to skip to the good part?"

"What's the good part?" I gaze at him as his hands are now on top of mine. We both crouch to put the basket down, and he opens it, taking out the letter. He stands, and opens it.

"I have adored you for the longest time," he reads out while I stand, taking a few steps back. "There you have it, Nathan. The clue was every first word from the sixteenth letter. I bet you didn't get that, now did you? If you did, congratulations, you've won. Now all I need to know is–"

"Do you have feelings for me as well?" I whisper, taking a deep breath.

Nathan closes the letter, then casts it aside, his eyes on me. For the first time, I can't read the look on his face, nor can I tell by the body language what he's about to do. He's rigid, his eyes full of an emotion I cannot decipher, and his stance unwavering. At last, he steps over the basket and approaches me, getting as physically close as he possibly can.

"Since the first letter, Leon," he whispers, his hands cupping my cheeks. "And my affection for you only grew once I got to know you a bit more. I like you, Leon. I've always liked you. I told you that you were my home, remember? Or did you think I was lying?"

"I thought you said that to make me feel better about myself," I admit.

"There's nothing that I can say to make you feel better when you already know how special you are to me," Nate replies, his forehead resting against mine. "Perhaps the only way to convince you is to show you."

He caresses my cheek lightly, and brings me closer to him, our lips barely touching.

"You're nervous," Nathan whispers in my ear. "I'm here, there's nothing to be afraid of. It's just you and me."

I take a deep breath and close my eyes. "You and me," I repeat.

He then takes this chance to try and kiss me again, but this time, I allow it.

I smile against his lips and wrap my arms around his neck, melting into him. He keeps me steady, his lips off of mine in an instant as we stand in the middle of the garden, holding each other as the sun slowly disappears from the horizon. He pushes back my curls and kisses the top of my forehead, hugging me tight.

"I wish I could've done more," I mumble. "I was just so afraid. I didn't want you to fall in love with the words on the paper."

"This was perfect, and you know why?" Nathan asks.

"Why?"

"Because you told me how *you* wanted to tell me. And no, I did not fall in love with the words. I instead saw the person behind them." We let go of each other and he smiles down at me. "Well, it is getting a bit late, don't you think?"

"Yeah, you're right." I nod, taking him by the hand. "Lion King?"

Nathan squeezes my hand tightly. "Lion King."

Chapter 35: Three Weeks Later

"I never thought I'd see the day that we'd end up at Nathan's house watching them outdo each other in chess," Derek jokes as we wait for Nathan to make a move.

"Well, surprises are common when you hang out with people like me," Nate finally moves his bishop. "Isn't that right, Lee?"

"What surprise have you given me since we've known each other?" I raise my eyebrows.

"The gift of friendship," Nate answers.

"Yeah right." Yvonne rolls her eyes. "Friends don't hide behind the bleachers just to make out."

"Nor do they walk around school hand in hand just to piss people off," Derek adds.

"And they don't post pictures of them kissing on their instagram stories either," Cecelia chimes in.

"Okay, maybe we are more than friends," I admit. "Is it a crime to show off?"

"Yes, it is," Yvonne says. "Especially if you got the most desirable guy ever."

"In tenth grade," Derek corrects her. "And one of them, might I add."

"The only person that wants you is the principal because you've been acting a mess during assembly again." Cecelia snickers.

Yvonne comes to Derek's defence. "At least he's *wanted*. You on the other hand—"

Nathan and I shake our heads simultaneously before continuing the game as the 3 of them start to bicker.

It's been 3 weeks since we started dating, and three weeks since we publicly came out to the school. It wasn't a big deal to the school anyway, because nobody really cares about the next person as much as they claim to, but to me, it meant everything. It was the first time I could feel free and happy, without anyone breathing down my neck or judging me for who I am. And to be honest,

I don't think I would've done it if it wasn't for my friends, and for Nathan giving me the courage and strength to carry on.

In one way or the other, I may have also helped Nathan become more open to different things. He finally joined the chess team, as well as began training twice as hard to be captain next year. Nathan did leave his friend group to join ours, and by the looks of it, he's happy.

He's happy.

Nathan silently puts me in checkmate before pointing to the kitchen. He mouths the words 'let's go' and I nod, slipping away from our friends.

When we're in the kitchen, Nathan reaches into his pocket, and hands me a piece of paper. "Can you guess what it is?"

I grin. "Let me guess; a letter?"

"Perhaps, or maybe an eviction note?" He asks. "Because I can't get you out of my mind–"

"Hey, leave the bad jokes to me," I laugh, the paper in my hands shaking. "Can I open it?"

"It's yours, of course you can."

Staring at him one more time, I open the letter, and begin to read.

• • ❧ • •

HE WROTE LETTERS TO me. And now, this is my letter to him.

Hey Lee. Or J, or should I say babe? Either way, it doesn't matter what I call you. The meaning behind it stays the same, as always.

Now, I'm not too good with words. I don't have a fancy nickname for you like the one you gave me in one of your letters. I'm no God, I'm no angel, and I'm certainly not the King you set me out to be. But in your eyes, you see that. How you see me matters most to me, and now that you've told me how I look in your eyes, it's time I tell you how you look in mine.

If I'm being perfectly honest, you're a diamond, an emerald, and all the precious little things in the world combined. As timeless as your letters will be since they're in my chest cabinet, my awe for you will never fade. I wish I could say everything that I've ever thought about you in my head, but I can't, I simply don't have the words to describe how much you mean to me.

Talk to you soon, Lee.

Nathaniel ♡

WITHOUT HESITATION, I jump on him, hugging him as he spins us around. He puts me down and pats my head. "I'm not a poet like you, so please bear with me."

"You don't have to be a poet," I say, the tears in my eyes blurring my vision. "You just need to be yourself. Be Nate."

"As long as you'll always be Leon." He hugs me once more before we head back to the others, hand in hand.

Cece and Yvonne were currently wrestling for the last bag of chips while Derek watched on, amused. Realising that we're back in the room, Cecelia throws the bag of chips in my direction, then pushes Yvonne off of her.

"Leo, run!"

"Nope, keep it between yourselves!" Nathan snatches the packet from my hands and throws it at Yvonne, who immediately tears it open. "You're welcome."

"At least you're on my side. Derek was too busy siding with his ex," Yvonne scoffs, rolling her eyes at him.

"Okay, you win." Cecelia grumbles, walking over to Yvonne, who presses the bag against her chest. "Sharing is–"

"For five year olds," Yvonne interjects. "But, because I like you, I'll give you some."

"Wait, you like her?" Derek wriggles his eyebrows.

"Do you like her?" Nathan asks Derek.

"No, Yvonne's my friend, and so is Cece. The question is for the ladies." He points at Cece and Yvonne, the duo letting go of each other's hands. "Do you like each other?"

"No!" They both yell, but Cecelia's pink cheeks and Yvonne's averted gaze are telling a different story.

Derek and I look at each other, then back at the pair. I think it's time Derek 'works his magic' one more time, right? If it worked for Nathan and I, despite the challenges and the duration, it can work for Cecelia and Yvonne.

Derek clears his throat as we anxiously wait for him to say something. Once he's done clearing it, he stands up, winks at Nathan and I, then looks at Cecelia and Yvonne;

"Wanna bet?"

Did you love *22 Letters*? Then you should read *Ordinary Human Beings*[1] by Salem Miles!

[2]

"This year was supposed to be about me being out of the spotlight and minding my own business, not about me French kissing one of the school's most hated kids in the back of the burner room!" Yasmina shut the door in my face."You better not lock—" the click was loud enough for me to roll my eyes. "The door."***After a controversial start to the New Year, Kendall Riddick has to navigate her first senior year at Riveria Boarding School while trying to avoid her ex girlfriend and former best friend on campus. But none of that is easy, as a not so unfamiliar stranger decides to enrol into the school...and guess what? She's Kendall's room-mate. And if there's one thing Kendall has learned about sharing a room with a complete 'stranger' is that room-mates don't kiss, right?

Right?

---

1. https://books2read.com/u/4DJzDe

2. https://books2read.com/u/4DJzDe

Also by Salem Miles

22 Series
22 Letters

Riveria Series
Ordinary Human Beings

About the Author

Born in South Africa but raised in Zimbabwe, Salem Miles is a young adult author that has passion for the written craft. She started writing when she was just 14, and since then, she has dedicated herself to writing stories that makes everyone feel heard and seen. During her freetime, she likes to spend her day with her loved ones, preferably drinking coffee and eating a baguette in the process.